THE MASKED MARKSMAN:
TOP BILLING FOR MURDER
AND OTHER STORIES

THE MASKED MARKSMAN

TOP BILLING
FOR MURDER
AND OTHER STORIES

By Emile C. Tepperman

POPULAR PUBLICATIONS • 2025

PUBLISHING HISTORY

"Murder Misses Its Cue" originally appeared in the September, 1937 (Vol. 12, No. 4) issue of *The Spider* magazine. "Dead Man's Bullets" originally appeared in the December, 1937 (Vol. 13, No. 3) issue of *The Spider* magazine. "Corpse Without a Coffin" originally appeared in the March, 1938 (Vol. 14, No. 2) issue of *The Spider* magazine. "The Corpse Takes a Curtain Call" originally appeared in the April, 1938 (Vol. 14, No. 3) issue of *The Spider* magazine. "Murder Matinee" originally appeared in the May, 1938 (Vol. 14, No. 4) issue of *The Spider* magazine. "Death Books the Show" originally appeared in the June, 1938 (Vol. 15, No. 1) issue of *The Spider* magazine. "Top Billing for Murder" originally appeared in the July, 1938 (Vol. 15, No. 1) issue of *The Spider* magazine. Copyright 2025 by Argosy Communications, Inc. All rights reserved.

MURDER MISSES ITS CUE

ED RACE stopped stock-still, every nerve taut, every muscle alert. The kid—he was hardly more than nineteen at the outside—had slipped out of the shadows of the alley between two dark warehouses, and the gun he pointed at Ed seemed to be doing a parabola in the air.

"Lift up your hands," the kid ordered. "I want your money!"

Ed was poised on the balls of his feet, hands half-raised, on a level with the two .45 caliber revolvers that nestled in his own shoulder-clips—.45's that could do him no good now, for the kid's gun muzzle was less than six inches from his chest. And, though the kid's hand was shaking as with the ague, there wasn't a chance in ten million that he could miss if he fired.

"You're pretty young," Ed said mildly, "to be pulling stuff like this. You could get thirty years—"

"Never mind!" the kid snarled. He poked the gun closer. "Stand still. I'd just as soon plug you as not. They want me for murder already. They can't hang me twice!"

The young fellow had no jacket, and no necktie. His once white shirt was filthy, and a downy stubble of blond beard showed on his chin. His hair was matted, and there was a deep, open gash in his right cheek, from which fresh blood was still trickling.

Ed's eyes narrowed. He watched the kid's eyes. They were

He swung into action instantly.

desperate. This youngster would surely shoot. Yet Ed Race couldn't afford to allow himself to be held up this way. It would ruin him, make him the laughingstock of the vaudeville circuits and of the wiseacre columnists back in New York.

Ed Race was the masked marksman of vaudeville fame. Throughout the country he was billed wherever he appeared, as "The Man Who Can Make Guns Talk!" His vaudeville number consisted of an acrobatic juggling act in which he used six hair-trigger .45 caliber revolvers instead of the usual dumb-bells. His feats of marksmanship with them generally left the audience goggling with admiration. Two of those hair-trigger revolvers were in his shoulder-clips now. He could imagine how they would laugh along the Main Stem, when the news got out that Ed Race had been held up by a kid with a gun!

And if the kid should take his two revolvers in addition to his wallet, that would be the crowning indignity—because Ed needed those two guns to go on with his performance at the Blountsville Theater tomorrow.

The kid's finger was curled about the trigger of the gun, and the gun was still wavering in the air, close to Ed's chest. With his left hand the kid reached toward Ed's breast pocket.

"Is this where you keep your money?" he demanded. "Better hand—"

"Wait a minute!" Ed broke in. The light from the single street lamp down at the corner had just given him a deep glimpse into the young fellow's eyes, and he had seen there only innocence and wild desperation. They were clear blue, not vicious, not scheming or shrewd.

"Did you say you're wanted for murder?"

The boy's lips pouted, and he momentarily lowered his eyes. "Yes," he whispered. "And I'll kill again if I have to."

Ed smiled suddenly. He knew human nature all too well. The kid was lying. "I'm not giving you my wallet!" he said deliberately. "Now let's see what kind of cold-blooded murderer you are. *Pull that trigger!*"

ED WAS taut, cold with suspense. He was gambling his life on his judgment. These were the things that made life worth while to Ed Race—excitement, peril, high risk. His vaudeville contract brought him enough money so that he did not have to worry for the rest of his life. But that restless something that has made adventurers of men in all the ages of the world, would not let him be content. Ed needed danger and thrill as other men need food. In search of that element of risk, Ed Race had found himself an avocation—that of criminology. He was licensed in a dozen states as a private detective, and he had often used those licenses in sharp encounters with crime. If his experience qualified him as a judge of criminals then he was ready to stake his life that this lad was no murderer.

The boy hesitated for the fraction of a second. His finger tightened on the trigger of the gun that was pointed at Ed's chest. Ed could almost feel the white-hot streak of the slug that would tear through him if the kid's finger tightened a sixteenth of an inch.

But it didn't tighten.

Abruptly, the boy uttered a choked groan that was more like a muted sob of hopelessness. His finger uncurled from the trigger, and he lowered the gun.

"I—I can't!" he sobbed. "I—can't!"

He flung the gun from him, and covered his face with his hands. The gun clattered on the cold concrete, making a terrifically loud noise in the stillness of the deserted street. And just then the sound of screeching tires came from around the corner.

The lad looked up in alarm, tears streaking his cheeks. He glanced at Ed. "It's a police car! For God's sake, mister, don't let them get me. They won't give me a chance—"

He stopped, his eyes widening, as an open car swung into the riverfront street. The car's spotlight bathed both Ed and the boy in its merciless glare. A voice shouted, "There's the Blount kid! *Shoot him down!*"

The two occupants of the patrol car were not in uniform, but the street lamp showed the glitter of their police badges, pinned to the outside of their coats. Ed had gathered from the lad's incoherent remarks that he was being hunted. Perhaps he had escaped from custody.

It was the driver who had shouted the order to shoot the boy down. The second man in the car held a sub-machine gun, and he raised the weapon to obey the command.

Ed's lips tightened in a grim line. Those officers could plainly see that the boy was unarmed. Yet they were ready to cut him down without giving him a chance to surrender. Also, in the process, they would shoot down Ed Race. Manifestly, they preferred to bring this boy in dead rather than alive.

The car had come to a stop within twenty feet of them, and the sub-machine gun was raised halfway to the officer's shoulder. Ed Race could see the man's cold, ruthless eyes over the sights.

The boy screamed, "Don't shoot! I—"

Ed didn't wait for the lad to make his plea. He knew that no plea would help. He could read the deadly determination in the officers' faces.

On the stage, when performing with his heavy .45's, the Masked Marksman always astounded his audiences with the swift, symphonic sureness of his movements. Now he swung into action with that same lightning swiftness. The motion of his two hands was so fast that no human eyes could have followed them. But suddenly, miraculously, the two .45's leaped from their shoulder-clips as if released by springs.

The left hand gun remained upright in the air, while the right hand one leveled, and roared once. The big gun bucked in Ed's hand as flame spat from its muzzle. A slug whined, and the officer with the sub-machine gun seemed to have been slapped backward by a mighty tornado of wind.

The reverberation of the shot echoed back along the river-front, drowning the officer's scream. The sub-machine gun dropped from numbed fingers, and the man clapped a hand to his shoulder, his face gone suddenly white with pain. Ed had shot him just where he wanted to—high in the shoulder.

The man at the wheel was struggling to get his own gun, and Ed called to him coldly, "Don't try it, mister!"

The fellow dropped his hand.

THE BOY was sweating profusely, staring with wide, almost unbelieving eyes at the little trickle of smoke from Ed's revolver muzzle. "You shot him!" he kept saying. "You shot—" His voice was shaky.

Ed nodded grimly. "It was either that, or get shot, myself. There's something wrong with this set-up, kid. I've never seen police officers so quick to shoot down an unarmed man. Let's look them over quick—before more of them come."

He stepped swiftly toward the car, keeping the driver covered. The wounded man was groaning, pressing a handkerchief against his bloody shoulder.

"Don't worry," Ed Race told him. "You won't die of that."

The driver of the car snarled at him; "Mister, you walked into something. Your life won't be worth two cents in Blountsville after this!"

Ed grinned at him. "Thanks for the warning. Now let's take a look at that badge!"

He reached across the wounded man, unpinned the driver's badge, and held it up where the light shone on it. He nodded grimly.

"Just as I thought. I knew you weren't police officers!"

The badge read, *Jordane Detective Agency, Blountsville, Operator 17.*

"You see, kid," he said to the lad, who was peering over his shoulder, "they're just rats. No decent policeman would shoot down a man without a gun."

The kid gasped, "I knew it, I knew it! King Jordane wants to wipe out our whole family!"

"What's your name, kid?" Ed demanded.

"Freddie Blount."

"Okay, Freddie. I think you need a friend. Here"—he holstered one of his guns, and reached into his pocket, pulled out a wad of bills—"here's the money you wanted. Did you have a particular place to go to?"

7

Freddie Blount took the money with a shaking hand. "Y-yes. I was going to—"

"Don't say it in front of these eggs!" Ed snapped. He backed away, out of earshot, still keeping the driver of the car covered, while the wounded man continued to groan.

"Now, tell me."

"My father owns a small hotel about four miles out on the state highway. I could get in the back way, and hide in the cellar—"

"What's the name of this hotel?"

"Blount's Inn."

"All right. Can you drive?"

"Yes."

Ed nodded. "Fine." He waved his gun at the car. "Will you gentlemen kindly get out of there?"

The driver hesitated, and Ed said coldly; "The two of you are a couple of rats, and I'd enjoy putting a nice slug in you, to match the one in your pal's shoulder. Now, *move fast!*"

THEY BELIEVED him. The driver helped his companion out to the sidewalk, and Ed motioned the boy into the car, then got in beside him, being careful not to touch the spots where blood from the wounded man's shoulder had dripped on the seat. He reached out, thrust his hand under the driver's coat, and took out the man's gun. "All right, Freddie," he said. "Let's go!"

Freddie shot the gear into first, pulled the car away. The street was still deserted. No one had come at the sound of Ed's shot. If anyone had heard it, it had probably been mistaken for the backfire of an automobile.

"Drop me off at the next corner," Ed ordered. "Go to that hotel, and stay there till you hear from me. I'm going to find out what's at the bottom of all this."

The boy's hands tightened on the wheel. "Y-you're going to help me?"

"Yes."

"B-but you don't even know me. And I'm wanted for murder. You're in trouble already. Jordane is powerful in Blountsville. He'll scour the city for you. And if you help me, you'll be an accessory after the fact—to murder!"

"Tell me one thing, kid," Ed asked quietly. *Are you guilty of murder?"*

"God," Freddie Blount gulped. "I—don't know!"

They were at the edge of town now, and heading for the open road. "Drive on," Ed told him. "I'll take the car back from the hotel, so they won't trace you."

Sirens were screaming in the town behind them. Soon the manhunt would be on in earnest.

"Now talk fast," Ed said to the boy. "Tell me the whole thing from the beginning."

"All right." Freddie kept his hands tight on the wheel, his eyes on the road ahead. Ed might have taken the wheel, but he thought that the effort of driving would serve to steady the lad's nerves. "Go ahead with the story," he encouraged him.

"Well, my father once owned all of Blountsville, practically. He's Harold Blount, you know."

Ed Race drew in a sharp breath. He might have guessed it when he first heard Freddie's name. He, himself, the Masked

Marksman, was scheduled to appear at the Blount Theater tomorrow. He had met Harold Blount earlier in the day, as well as Blount's pretty young daughter, Mary. Both of them had appeared overwrought, in the grip of some deep emotion. But Ed had not tried, then, to pry into their trouble. It was this business of Freddie's that must have been preying on their minds.

FREDDIE BLOUNT was going on with the story. "Dad lost almost everything in the crash, and a syndicate from New York bought him up. All he had left was the Blount Theater, and the hotel out here. King Jordane moved into town shortly after that, and he's been running Blountsville to suit himself. He hates Dad, because Dad has been fighting him for years; and he's trying hard to break Dad, to take the theater from him."

"Snap it up!" Ed commanded. "Get down to cases. What about this murder charge?"

Freddie shuddered. "I was an awful fool!" he groaned. "I've been playing the dice table at Larkey's Place, on Maxwell Street. Jordane owns it, and I should have known better. That's one of the reasons why Dad's been fighting Jordane. Well, I got into an argument with the houseman at the table, and I knocked him down. He got up, going for his gun, and someone pushed a revolver into my hand. I didn't want to shoot, but the fellow who handed me the revolver squeezed my hand, and the gun went off. The houseman doubled up, and dropped to the floor, and then the lights went out. Someone hustled me out of the place, and I found myself in the street. I was dazed, and I didn't know what to do first, so I went home. When I got there, they were waiting for me. They took me to jail, charged with murder."

"I see," Ed said thoughtfully. "And you broke out?"

"Yes. I was arrested yesterday. This evening I learned that the body of the house man who was killed, had disappeared. They're looking for his body all over the city; but I understand they wouldn't even need the body to try me for murder. There are plenty of witnesses who saw the house man drop, and my lawyer tells me that would constitute a *corpus delicti*. Besides, Jordane owns the town, and he could pack a jury. I'd be sure to hang. So tonight, when I found my cell door had been left open by accident, I stole out. They had me in a separate wing, and the guard must have gone out for a minute. Nobody stopped me. I found a gun lying on the table in the office, so I took it. You know what happened after that."

Ed Race was frowning. "The body disappeared, eh? And they opened the door for you, so you could escape? You know, Freddie, they *wanted* you to escape—so they could shoot you down when they found you!"

Freddie Blount gasped. "I never thought of that!"

The bright headlights of the car picked up the outline of a white-painted, Colonial building, some two hundred feet back from the road.

"That's the hotel," Freddie said. "It's closed now, but I can get in."

"All right. Pull up here, and get out. How will I be able to reach you?"

"The place is closed up, but there's a public telephone in the lobby. Information will give you the number."

"Okay. Stick close to that 'phone."

Freddie Blount delayed getting out of the car. "Y-you've been pretty good to me—considering that you're a stranger. And I don't even know your name—"

"We're not exactly strangers, Freddie," Ed said softly. "You see, I know your old man. He used to have a small circuit of vaudeville theaters, years ago, and it was he who gave me my first start in the show business. I'm Ed Race."

Freddie Blount's eyes opened wide. "Why, sure! I've heard Dad mention your name many times. The Masked Marksman! That explains how you beat that tommy-gun!"

Ed pushed him gently out of the car. "Scram, kid. I've got work to do tonight. There's one thing more I'd like to know. What was the name of this houseman at Larkey's that you are supposed to have shot?"

"I don't know his last name. But they called him Pinky."

"Pinky? Was he a stocky chap, black pompadour, pink cheeks, bad teeth?"

"That's him, Mr. Race!"

Ed nodded. "Pinky Snell—one of the crookedest rats in the gambling racket. Larkey is a New York crook, too. Looks like your friend, Jordane, has brought in a bunch of big-timers to take Blountsville over!"

"Y-you think you can do something, Mr. Race?"

"I hope so. I'm going to stop at the theater and tell your Dad that you're still okay. And I want some information from him. Stick close to the 'phone in there!"

Ed turned the car around in the road, and headed back toward town.

BLOUNTSVILLE WAS a town of about eighteen thousand population, and its single main thoroughfare ran east and west, at right angles to the highway, which bisected the town. The Blount family had owned most of the town from its early days, when Abner Blount had opened the first general store to take care of the trade that came down the river from St. Louis. Later, the railroad, coming in, had given the town a second lease on life, and many manufacturing establishments had opened up here.

Ordinarily, Ed Race did not play a location as small as this, but the Partages Vaudeville Circuit, for which he worked, had found it necessary to fill in with a week or two in second-rate spots rather than bring Ed back to New York.

Now, Ed could see the Blount Theater, at the corner of Maxwell and Post. It was past midnight, and most of the lights were out along the street. The Blount ran a Sunday motion-picture show, because vaudeville was forbidden on Sunday by local ordinance. The last of the patrons were filing out, and the porter was up on a ladder alongside the marquee, setting up the signs for next week's show.

As Ed parked, he could read the words the man had already set up—

SPECIAL APPEARANCE
THE MASKED MARKSMAN
"THE MAN WHO CAN MAKE GUNS TALK"

They were billing him as the star attraction for the week. But there was a far greater attraction going on under the very noses of Blountsville—the drama of a young man being railroaded for murder, and of an old man being shoved out of the last of his family possessions by a ruthless crowd from the big city, led by a man with no mercy—King Jordane.

Ed Race had never met King Jordane personally, but he had heard many stories about the man. His lips pursed tightly. Jordane had the reputation of being dangerous and brave—and without conscience. He seemed to be riding in the saddle here in Blountsville. Ed wondered whether he, himself, was not setting out to buck a combination that might be just a little too big to handle.

He left the car, and entered the darkened theater, taking the stairs to the balcony floor, where he knew the office was located.

The place was dark, gloomy. The cleaning women had not come yet, and the last of the patrons had departed. The motion-picture operator had closed his booth and left. A streak of light came from under the office door, which was almost directly beneath the booth.

The sounds of low-voiced conversation came to Ed through the door. He raised a hand and knocked, and the voices ceased. There was a moment of silence, then a man called out, "Come!"

Ed frowned. That was not the voice of Harold Blount. Also, there was an edge to that voice which he did not like. He put a hand on the knob, turned it and thrust, at the same time raising his right hand so that his fingers touched the butt of the revolver under his left armpit.

He pushed the door open, himself remaining on the outside. The door swung away from him, revealing three persons in the

14

office within. One was young Mary Blount, sitting behind the desk in the corner, with her white hands flat on the glass top. Her face was flushed, her breasts rising and falling swiftly with the strain of great emotion.

Ed spared her only a glance. His eyes focused on the two masked men, with drawn guns, who were facing the doorway. One of them was squat, heavily built; the other was tall, lithe. They both wore slouch hats, with masks that covered their faces from hat-brim to chin. The squat one held a leather satchel under one arm, while his gun pointed unwaveringly at Ed Race. The taller one kept Mary Blount covered.

The squat man said sneeringly: "Hell, it's Ed Race in person! Glad I got the drop on you this time. Come on in, and be sociable."

Ed did not move his hand from its position touching the butt of his gun. Slowly, his eyes bleak, he entered the room.

THE TALL man grunted, walked around in back of the squat one, and kicked the door shut. The squat man spoke again. "We was just leaving, Race. Be good now, an' don't pull that gun of yours. No matter how fast you are, I could put a slug in your heart before you got it out!"

Ed's eyes burned into the mask. "I know you," he said deliberately. "You're—"

The taller man swiveled toward him, thrust out his gun. "You say that name, and I'll kill you!"

Ed shrugged. "I don't have to say it. I know it. And I see you're up to a little stick-up business." His eyes flicked to the leather wallet under the arm of the squat man, whose name he had been about to mention. "What's in there—the day's proceeds of the Blount Theater?"

"Yeah," said the squat man. "And it's too bad that you had to poke your nose in this. You say you know me. Well, take a tip, Race, and keep it to yourself. Forget you thought you knew me, see? You'll live longer!"

Throughout all this, Mary Blount had sat quietly, her eyes fixed on Ed Race. Her lips were trembling, as if she wanted to tell him something, but did not dare.

"Just a minute, my friends," Ed said mildly. "Don't go yet. I'm sorry, but I can't let you leave with that money. It's my guess that Miss Blount here was going to use the money to hire lawyers and so forth, for the defense of her brother. She needs the money, and it's going to stay here. You boys know me. I'm the Masked Marksman. If you've ever seen me on the stage, you know that I can draw a gun pretty fast."

Both men hesitated. Every word that Ed Race had said was true. They had only to pull the triggers of their guns to drill Ed Race. But they had both seen the Masked Marksman on the stage. They had both heard of the exploits of Ed Race off the stage. And they knew that he would surely get one of them.

The squat man's eyes plainly showed his fear.

The taller man reached a decision first. He glanced at Mary Blount. "Miss Blount," he said, "tell this fool not to interfere!"

Ed did not see Mary's face, but he heard her swallow audibly. After a second's hesitation, her voice came huskily.

"It—it's all right, Mr. Race. P-please let them go."

"Let them go!" Ed exclaimed incredulously. "With the

money? Oh, no. That money belongs to the theater. Where's your father?"

"He—he's home sick. He—he had a stroke tonight. And it's all right about the money. I—I *gave* it to them!"

"You—what?"

"I—gave them the satchel of money. And now, please let them go."

Ed's mind worked swiftly, puzzledly. She was lying, of course. These men had robbed her of the day's proceeds. They were masked. And the squat man....

Suddenly, Ed smiled. "Okay, Miss Blount, if you say so. It's your money." He shrugged, let his hand drop.

An audible sigh of relief came from under the mask of the squat fellow.

"An' now, Race, if you wanna be smart, forget what you said about knowin' me. You was mistaken, see?"

The taller one got the door open, and they backed out.

Ed swung on Mary Blount. "Why did you say that you had given them the money?" he demanded.

She was sobbing out loud now. "I—I had to. That tall man was King Jordane, himself. He told me my brother, Freddie, escaped from jail. And Jordane's operatives have been deputized by the sheriff. They have orders to shoot Freddie on sight. Jordane promised to countermand the order, if I didn't raise any trouble about the money—"

"Your brother is safe!" Ed broke in harshly.

He swung to the door, tore it open. The balcony was in darkness. He could hear the heavy tread of the two fleeing men as they sped down the stairs.

ED LEAPED after them. He rounded the first bend in the stairs, saw them both below, making for the side door.

They raised their guns, and flame spurted from both muzzles. Ed was moving fast, and the slugs whistled past him, whining in his ears. His own two guns came out even as he ran, and he fired from the hip, once with each gun.

Almost in unison, both men were hurled backward against the paneling of the fire-door. Their guns dropped, their hands waved wildly, and they collapsed. He reached the orchestra floor, ran toward the two inert bodies, with the thunderous reverberations of the shooting still ringing in his ears.

A police whistle was shrilling outside, as he knelt beside them.

Mary Blount came running down the stairs, stood beside him.

"Y-you've killed them both! But now Freddie—they'll shoot Freddie on sight—"

She was interrupted by the arrival of the patrolman on the beat, who came barging in, still red in the face from blowing his whistle. He saw the bodies.

"Robbers, huh?" he commented. "Who shot them?"

"I did," Ed said.

The patrolman glanced up at him, then knelt and removed the masks. He whistled. "Holy mackerel! This is King Jordane, himself!"

"And the other," Ed told him slowly, "is really a chap who died twice. Take his mask off."

The patrolman frowned, pulled the mask off the squat man. The officer shook his head. "Don't recognize him."

Ed grinned thinly. "That's the corpse that disappeared—Pinky Snell, in person. That's the man whom Freddie Blount is accused of murdering!"

The officer got to his feet, a dazed look in his face. "Then Freddie Blount didn't kill no one?"

"That's the idea, officer. They were keeping Pinky Snell out of the way, till they could catch Freddie and shoot him. Their idea was to kill him while he was still a fugitive from justice. That would make his killing legal. Afterward, it wouldn't matter if Pinky Snell returned to the land of the living; Freddie Blount would be dead! They planned it all."

Mary Blount, behind Ed, uttered a gasp. "T-then it was all framed up—the fight in Larkey's and the shooting?"

"Of course. They wanted a legal excuse for killing Freddie. And by relieving you of the day's proceeds here, they knew they'd put you in a hole, so you'd have to borrow money. They could take the theater away from your father, and King Jordane would own the whole town!"

"Glory be!" exclaimed the cop. "I don't know your name, mister, but every honest cop in Blountsville will be thankin' ye!"

"The name," Ed said with a smile, "is the Masked Marksman. Come and see the show tomorrow night—with the compliments of the house!"

DEAD MAN'S BULLETS

THE TRAIN jolted around a curve, and the fat man sitting next to Ed Race was almost precipitated into his lap. When the trail straightened out, Ed rearranged his newspaper, which had been crumpled in the tangle. The fat man had been smoking a fat cigar, and its ashes were all over Ed's trousers.

Ed nodded in recognition of his neighbor's profuse apologies.

"These damned day coaches, sir! There ought to be a law against them. I'll be glad when I get to Torrid City. My name's Beglin, sir—Amos Beglin." The fat man smiled, a bit nervously. "I see you're going to Torrid City, too." He glanced at Ed's ticket, which was inserted into the upholstery in the seat in front of them.

Ed hadn't given his neighbor much attention during the trip from Philadelphia. Now, he turned to look at him. "Yes," he told Mr. Amos Beglin. "I'm headed for Torrid City, too. They say it's as hot as its name."

Beglin applied a match to his cigar. His hand was shaking so that the flame flickered. "Damn it!" he exclaimed peevishly. "I'm nervous as a radio amateur." He tried a second match, got the cigar going. "You see, I'm a witness in that Clay Manning murder case. It goes on today, and the defense lawyer 'phoned me to come right up from Philly."

Ed Race tensed. "You—you're a defense witness?" he asked.

"That's right. I'm Clay Manning's boss. Prosecutor Kedrick contends that Clay Manning shot Hilda Worth at eight o'clock in the evening on September twentieth. Well, at eight o'clock that night, I was talking to Clay on the long distance. I got him at his hotel—the Empire. You see, if he was talking to me at eight, he couldn't have been out at the Worth place, which is forty miles from Torrid City. My testimony will clear Clay absolutely!"

Ed Race's eyes were bright. "That's good news to me, Mr. Beglin. My name is Race. I'm a good friend of Clay Manning. I was coming out to testify for him as a character witness."

Amos Beglin smiled broadly. "Why, of course! I've heard Clay talk about you. You're the vaudeville star who juggles guns on the stage, and knocks their eyes out with your marksmanship. They call you 'The Masked Marksman.' I've seen you a dozen times—in fact, I go every time you play Philly. But I didn't recognize you on account of that mask you always wear on the stage."

ED RACE smiled. He was used to the admiration of the public. His headline vaudeville number was familiar to theater-goers from coast to coast. He juggled six heavy .45 caliber revolvers on the stage, with the ease with which another might have juggled dumbbells. And he received enough in salary from the Partages Circuit to live comfortably and to bank large sums every year. But there was a restless something within him which did not permit him to rest upon that success. His nervous energy craved other outlets—outlets in which danger would play a predominant part. So, he had chosen for himself an avocation

Ed Race's big gun was roaring
out its message of death!

that would satisfy that craving for danger. He dabbled in criminology on the side.

He held licenses as a private detective in a dozen states,

and his name was hated in the underworld as much as he was admired in the vaudeville world. He always carried two of his hair-trigger .45's in shoulder holsters, and those fast-talking guns had blazed a reputation for Ed Race in the world of crime-fighting that was fully the equal of the Masked Marksman's reputation in the world of entertainment.

When Ed Race had heard that his friend, Clay Manning, was in serious trouble In Torrid City, he had 'phoned Manning's counsel, and taken the first train. The newspaper accounts of the case had given a pretty hopeless picture of Clay Manning's chances. But this meeting with Amos Beglin raised Ed's hopes.

It was apparent that John Stoneman, Manning's lawyer, had kept Beglin in the background, as a surprise witness. Now Ed smiled almost paternally at the fat man. "Let's stick together," he said. "It begins to look pretty good for Clay. I'd never believe he killed that girl."

THE TRAIN was slowing up, and the conductor came down the aisle announcing that the next stop was Torrid City. Amos Beglin motioned to the baggage-rack over their heads. "Would you mind, Mr. Race? I'm so damned fat, I can't do a thing for myself."

Ed smiled, and got up to reach down Beglin's tan suitcase, which was next to his own. And it was that little act of courtesy which probably saved his life....

Things happened fast.

He didn't see the telegraph messenger who came into the car, but he heard the boy calling, "Telegram for Mr. Beglin. Mr. Beglin—"

Amos Beglin motioned to the messenger. "Here, boy! I'm Mr. Beglin!"

Ed was lifting the valise off the rack, when he heard a gasp from behind him. Beglin's voice, suddenly thick with terror, followed the gasp. "Oh God, no—"

Ed turned his head automatically, while his hand balanced the tan suitcase.

Two men stood in the aisle, near the vestibule of the car. One had a revolver, the other carried a wicked, gleaming submachine gun under his arm. Both wore caps low down over their faces, and their coat collars were turned up. Ed could see eyes gleaming murderously under the peaks of those caps—eyes that were fixed upon Amos Beglin.

A scream welled in Amos Beglin's throat. "No, no! Don't shoot—"

And then the machine gun began to chatter, to buck in the grip of the gunner as he began to empty the clip into Beglin's body. Beglin screamed once, and then collapsed in the seat.

Ed Race reacted with the swift speed of a man who has been trained to meet danger and emergency. His hand fell away from the tan suitcase, which toppled down onto the seat in front. His right hand did not cease its downward movement, but snaked in and out from his shoulder holster, emerging with one of the .45's.

Slugs from that .45 smashed accurately into the faces of those two gunmen, crashing them backward into the vestibule. The machine gun flew upward from the dead, nerveless hands of its operator, while the second thug fell with a bullet in his forehead.

Women screamed in the car, and a police whistle shrilled somewhere outside.

Ed Race's eyes were bleak and cold. On the stage, he was called upon to give daily exhibitions of accurate shooting which left his audiences gasping with amazement. Had he remained sitting in the seat next to Beglin, some of the slugs from that machine gun would undoubtedly have smashed into his body. But he would still have managed to get those two gunmen.

HE DID not spare those two a second glance, for he knew where he had hit them. He whirled, bent, and peered out of the open window. Those two had boarded the train from the station, on the heels of the telegraph messenger. They must have accomplices in the station. Ed's narrowed eyes, darting across the station, spotted a long touring sedan. It was moving slowly up the street, alongside the station, and a face was framed in the side window—a face that was thin, saturnine, almost vicious.

The getaway car? He could not be sure. The sedan was crawling along, and its door swung open; the face disappeared from the window and a black-gloved hand reached out and pulled the door shut. Then the sedan slid smoothly away, turning the corner. Ed's glance darted to the license plate on the rear. It was indistinguishable, blurred with mud.

Ed turned from the window. He was morally certain that had been the getaway car for these two gunmen. But he couldn't shoot at it without more certainty. However, he'd not forget that face in the window. It was indelibly etched in his mind—a narrow, long head, thin lips, pointed chin, high flat ears, wearing a black derby hat....

Ed holstered his guns, let his glance drop to the seat beside him. There was a cold feeling within him. He was prepared for what he saw. The messenger boy lay on his back in the aisle, still, white face staring upward out of unseeing eyes. He had been almost cut in two by that merciless stream of machine gun slugs. And in the seat beside Ed, his quivering body jammed against Ed's knees, Amos Beglin was slumped. His head was bowed, double chin resting upon his bloody chest.

"I'm—done, Race. But you—paid off—for me. Thanks."

Ed placed a hand behind his neck, tried to support his head. "Take it easy, old man. We'll get you to a hospital."

"No—use. I'm—through. You—got to tell them my story. Tell them—I talked to Clay Manning—on 'phone—" his voice was growing weaker, lower—"on September twentieth—at the Empire Hotel, at—eight o'clock—evening, That'll—clear Clay...."

The words trailed off into a wheeze, a rattle—and then silence. Beglin's body stiffened, relaxed. He was dead.

Ed Race looked up bitterly to the two police officers and the ambulance interne who had pushed their way through the car. "Too late," he told them. Then he looked down at the dead man in his arms. "No, Amos Beglin," he said softly, "I haven't paid off for you in full, yet. There's going to be hell popping in Torrid City before your account is square!"

PROSECUTOR KEDRICK, District Attorney of Torrid County, was a tall man in his middle forties, with a high, ambitious forehead and a firm, pugnacious jaw. His eyes were hard, flint-like as they centered on Ed Race.

"And your story is," he was saying with a slightly sardonic tone of incredulity, "that Beglin lived just long enough to make this statement to you, and then he died? You want me to believe that?"

Ed Race stirred in his chair, across from Kedrick's desk. His jaw muscles bulged, and a little vein stood out on the right side of his forehead. He glanced around the room at the others present. There were two newspaper reporters, inconspicuous in a corner; there was an official stenographer, seated at one end of the desk; and John Stoneman, Clay Manning's lawyer, stood by the window. Stoneman had his back to the room, and was looking out across the courtyard toward the county jail opposite.

Ed Race did not take his eyes from the prosecutor's face. "I don't give a damn what you believe, Kedrick. That's exactly what happened. I'll remember Amos Beglin's every word, if I live to be a hundred. And that's what I'm going to tell the jury when Clay Manning goes on trial today!"

Kedrick smiled thinly. "I doubt if the judge will allow that statement to go to the jury, my friend. It's hearsay. You can't testify to what a third party told you—"

John Stoneman, the defense attorney, turned away from the window, faced the room. He was a calm man, with a mild and well modulated voice. "I think Mr. Race's testimony will be admissible, Kedrick," he said. "What Beglin told him was a statement made with the knowledge that he was dying—"

Kedrick grunted impatiently. "That would be true only of a confession."

Ed Race arose. The prosecutor broke off as he glimpsed the

look in Ed's eyes. Ed stood tall and lank, facing the district attorney. "Do you mean to say," he demanded of Kedrick, "that you will try to keep my evidence of Beglin's dying statement out of court? You must know damn well that Clay Manning didn't kill Hilda Worth. In spite of that knowledge, are you going to try to convict him? Are you going to try to keep from the jury evidence which might acquit him?" He glared.

Kedrick nodded. "My business is to prosecute," he clipped out. "I am not a judge of a defendant's guilt or innocence. My duty is to present everything that would tend to convict him in the eyes of the jury. And Stoneman's duty is to try to get him acquitted."

For a long minute, the eyes of the two men locked. At last, Ed Race said, "All right, Kedrick. I'm going to make a monkey of you. I'm going out into Torrid City and turn the town upside down. And I'm going to find the real murderer of Hilda Worth."

Stoneman broke in, "Now don't loose your temper, Mr. Race. Gay hasn't been convicted yet. With your testimony, I think we'll have a chance—"

"A chance!" Ed burst out. "Sure we'll have a chance. The jury ought to believe what I'll tell them. But I want Clay Manning to have more than a chance. I want him to go free, without a doubt. And in order to do that, I've got to find the real murderer!"

Kedrick shrugged. "As you choose, Mr. Race. I will not detain you in the shooting of those two gunmen on the train, as it was clearly a case of self-defense. But there is the question of your carrying concealed weapons—"

Ed grinned sourly. He fished a wallet from his pocket, and

slapped down two official papers upon Kedrick's desk. One was a license to carry a gun, the other a license permitting Ed Race to do business in the State of Pennsylvania as a private detective.

"You knew I had those," Ed told him coldly. "But if I weren't carrying them with me, you'd have used it as an excuse to detain me!"

Kedrick shrugged, spread his hands. "Merely a formality, Race. But you're free to go now."

"I'll want a pass," Ed said. "A pass to see Clay Manning."

"With pleasure," Kedrick assented. "No one can say that I'm unfair to a prisoner." He wrote out a pass, handed it across the desk. "And may I inquire just how you propose to go about catching this 'real' murderer, as you call him? It's nine o'clock. Clay Manning goes on trial at ten. You have only an hour—"

OVER KEDRICK'S shoulder, Ed caught John Stoneman's warning glance, accompanied by a swift shake of the head. Stoneman was trying to tell him not to answer Kedrick's question. But Ed deliberately disregarded the warning. "I'm going out to Hilda Worth's place," he informed the prosecutor. "I think I can promise you that I will have some startling information for the trial."

He said it knowingly, with a little touch of secrecy. And Kedrick frowned.

"If you have any leads or clues, Race, it is your duty to turn them over to the police—"

Ed laughed loud and harshly. "So that they can be buried? No, sir!"

He arose. "I'll be back while the trial is going on!"

John Stoneman accompanied him to the door. The two reporters started out also, and Kedrick called after them, "Graham! And you, Young! Remember you were here by courtesy only. Nothing in your papers until after the trial!"

The two reporters nodded.

Out in the corridor, Graham accosted Ed. "Excuse me, Mr. Race. "I'm Graham, of the *Star*. Do you really have something which will help you prove that someone else killed Hilda Worth?"

Ed Race nodded slowly. "Be in court," he said shortly. "You've got a surprise coming."

He left Graham staring after him, and took Stoneman's arm. "Let's go over and see Clay."

Stoneman looked worried. "You really haven't anything, have you, Race? You're bluffing about special information? You don't expect to find anything at Hilda Worth's place, do you?"

"Of course not. But I want everybody to know where I'm going this morning. Kedrick is worried that my testimony about Beglin's dying statement will acquit Clay. All right, if Kedrick is worried, the true murderer of Hilda Worth will also be worried. He may decide that it would be a good idea to stop me, the way Amos Beglin was stopped."

Stoneman gasped. "You mean—you think they'll go after you with machine guns?"

"I hope they will!" Ed said grimly. *"And I'm making it as easy as possible for them, by telling them where I'll be this morning!"*

THE INTERVIEW with Clay Manning was necessarily short, because the trial would start in less than an hour. Ed hadn't seen Clay for almost two years, and he was startled at the change in his friend.

Clay Manning had once shared vaudeville headlines with Ed Race. His voice, a deep full baritone, had enchanted audiences. But he had found that he could write as well as he could sing, and he had left the stage to become a feature writer for the Beglin Syndicate. His exposes of small-town rackets had attracted wide attention, though written under a pseudonym.

"I came to this town," he told Ed as they walked up and down in the prison corridor, "because I had a tip that Hilda Worth could give me information about a gambling racket that's being worked here in Torrid City. I checked in at the Empire, and Amos Beglin, who was my managing editor, 'phoned me at eight o'clock."

John Stoneman interrupted to explain, "That, Mr. Race, is the time which the coroner fixes as the hour when Hilda Worth was shot. That will be corroborated by a waitress in Hilda Worth's roadhouse, who will testify that she heard two shots at about eight o'clock, from Hilda's private office in the rear of the building. At the time, she thought it was the backfire of an automobile, and paid no attention."

"I see," said Ed. He turned to Manning. "What about Beglin's 'phone call, Clay? Won't the operator in the Empire corroborate it?"

Manning's eyes were etched with the dark lines of worry. "No, Ed. That girl has left town, apparently. She quit her job the day after the murder, and hasn't been seen since." He added bitterly, "Mr. Stoneman has put in a lot of work on this case, but, after all, he hasn't the facilities of the district attorney to trace missing witnesses."

Stoneman nodded. "And that will be a strong point for the prosecution in refutation of Beglin's dying testimony. I can just imagine Kedrick acidly telling the jury that, if Clay *did* talk on the 'phone at eight o'clock, we should have produced the telephone operator. And the rules of evidence won't even allow us to show the jury that the operator has disappeared!"

"I suppose the telephone company has a record of the call?" Ed asked.

"They have. But it doesn't prove that it was really Clay on the 'phone."

"All right," Ed said. "What happened after you got the 'phone call?"

Manning was smoking a cigarette nervously. "I drove out to Hilda Worth's. My car was parked in back of the Empire, and it's just my luck that no one saw me go out. Hilda Worth ran a road-house on the main highway—the Pigeon Inn. Its forty miles out. I had already talked to her on the 'phone, and she said she had information for me that would blow the whole county wide open.

"It seems that she was running a gambling room upstairs in the Pigeon Inn, and someone higher up was taking all her profits for protection. When she balked, they raided her, and pretty near destroyed the place. They ruined the fixtures, tables, kitchen, everything. It represented an investment of many thousands of dollars for her, and she was plenty sore. She was just managing to run the place with one waitress and a cook, until she could raise the money to make the necessary repairs. She told me on the 'phone to be careful and come in the back way, because she might be watched."

Ed nodded. "So you drove out there, and went in the back way—"

"And found Hilda Worth dead on the floor, with two slugs in the back of her head!" Manning crushed his cigarette viciously on the floor. "They knew I was coming out, Ed. They had the thing all framed and ready. The gun was on the floor. I didn't touch it, but the police found no prints. It had been wiped clean. I started to back out of there, and two State Troopers were waiting for me with drawn guns outside. Someone had 'phoned them, anonymously."

Ed Race pondered for a moment. "Don't you know anything at all about this gambling racket? Didn't Hilda Worth give you any hint on the 'phone? Didn't you talk about it to anyone here in Torrid City?"

"Hilda Worth didn't give me any dope on the 'phone. She only said she could tell me who was the top man that was getting the protection money. I talked to Kedrick when I first arrived in town. I asked him if he'd follow up any dope I got here on the gambling racket, but I didn't tell him from whom I was getting it. I also talked to Stan Ormsby, the publisher of the *Star*. He subscribes to the Beglin Syndicate, and I wanted to arrange with him to put the story on his presses the minute I got it. But I didn't tell him, either, where the information was coming from."

"I think I've got something to work on, Clay," Ed told him. "I'm going now. Mr. Stoneman, you try to prolong that trial as long as you can, till I get back." He shook hands with Clay Manning, and left with the lawyer.

THEY WENT through the courthouse from the jail, and Stoneman said, "I've got to get into the courtroom, Race. Good luck to you. But for God's sake, don't take too many chances. I need your testimony about Beglin's dying statement. Without that, we're licked cold—"

He broke off jerkily, as Ed gripped his arm hard. *"Who's that, coming out of Kedrick's office?"*

That face he would never forget—the long, narrow head, thin lips, pointed chin, high, flat ears. It was the face he had glimpsed in the touring-sedan outside the station. And here was its owner, walking out of Prosecutor Kedrick's office!

Stoneman threw a quick glance in that direction. He frowned. "Why, that's Flint Ormsby, Stan Ormsby's brother. Stan Ormsby is the publisher of the *Star*—the man Clay Manning was to give the story to when it broke. Flint Ormsby is on the district attorney's confidential staff. His brother got him the job."

"I see," Ed said softly. "I'm going, Stoneman. Be seeing you!"

He left the attorney, and walked swiftly toward the street, in the wake of the saturnine-faced Flint Ormsby. His elbows nudged his sides as he walked, bringing the two shoulder holsters forward under his coat, so that he could reach them with greater ease.

When he got to the door of the courthouse, he saw Flint Ormsby crossing the street, to enter the same touring-sedan that he had seen at the station. The sedan did not leave, but Ed could see the driver step on the starter. He could also see Ormsby's face in the rear. There were two more men in there with him, but they were keeping far back.

As he reached the sidewalk, a cab from the hack stand down at the corner pulled out of the line and braked at the curb in front of him. The driver grinned ingratiatingly. "Taxi, sir?"

Ed nodded. "Know where the Pigeon Inn is?" he asked.

"Yes, sir. Out on the highway—about forty miles. I'll make you a flat rate of five bucks. That all right with you?"

Ed raised his eyebrows. That was pretty cheap. "All right. Take me out there."

He got in, and the driver made a complete turn in the middle of the street, passing within a couple of feet of the touring-sedan as he turned. Ed, watching keenly, with both hands close to his guns, saw the driver make a slight signal with his hand. At once, the driver of the sedan gunned his motor, and leaped ahead, passing the cab. It headed swiftly up Main Street toward the open highway, with Ed's cab far behind.

Ed leaned back in his seat and smiled. They knew where he was going. They were going to wait until he got into the open country.

THE CAB left the town behind, and swung out into the open road. Ed glanced at the clock. The driver had not put the flag down, because he was making a special rate. He couldn't tell how far they had traveled, but he judged they were about fifteen miles out.

Ed leaned back once more. From the identification card, he noted that the cabby's name was Michael Pond. He waited while the cab rolled on for about another ten miles, watching constantly ahead for a sight of the touring-sedan.

The country was flat farm land here, with an occasional gas station or roadside stand. It was growing more and more lonely. Ed wondered if Ormsby would wait for him on the road, or go on to the Pigeon Inn to waylay him there. He decided not to take a chance on that.

He tapped on the glass. "Pull up at the side of the road," he ordered.

The driver did not stop. "We'll be there pretty soon, mister—"

"I said—*pull up!*" Ed rapped. His gun was out, boring into the back of Michael Pond's neck.

Pond squirmed under the feel of the cold metal. Ed could see, in the rear-vision mirror, that the man's eyes were narrowing. He tooled the cab to a halt at the side of the road. "W-what's the idea, mister?"

Ed said, "I'll show you. Just come in back. And do it quick!"

He emphasized the order with an additional poke of the gun, and Pond got out, came around and clambered into the rear compartment beside Ed. There was dawning dread in his eyes, and he kept his hands in the air.

Ed frisked him swiftly, and found a shiny .32 in his side coat pocket. He grinned at the man. "Since when do cab drivers carry those things?"

The driver opened his mouth to say something, thought better of it, and shut up. Ed took off the man's belt, and said, "Turn around, now."

"B-but what's the idea, mister? I don't get the idea."

"You'll get the idea—soon enough. Put your hands in back of you, and face the other way."

Pond obeyed, and Ed twisted the belt around the man's two wrists, then knotted it tightly. He pushed Pond over into a corner, then took off his own belt, and passed it under Pond's right armpit, attaching the other end to the rear-window handle. This served to keep the bound man erect in the rear seat. Now, Ed took off his own hat, put on the driver's cap, placing his hat on the driver.

Pond's eyes opened wide, and naked terror shown in them. "For Gawd's sake, don't do that, mister. They'll think I'm *you*— Look, let's move on while we—"

He bit the words off, realizing that he had said too much. He cowered into the corner.

Ed grinned thinly. "Now, you get the idea, Mr. Pond. *I'm* going to drive this hack. *You'll* be the passenger. When your friend, Flint Ormsby and his gang stop us, they'll spray this passenger compartment with lead. *You'll* get the slugs that will be intended for me!"

Michael Pond's mouth quivered. "Gawd, no!"

ED SAID nothing. He got in front, behind the wheel, and started the cab. He drove slowly, giving the bound man time to mull over his situation. They passed a gas station, went on for a couple of miles, and approached another. The silence was growing intense.

At last, the hoarse voice of Pond came from the rear. "Mister, I got a wife and two kids—"

Ed held the wheel tight. The man was beginning to break.

"That's too bad," he said. "You should have thought of that before you went in for murder. Murderers mustn't mind reverse English."

He slowed down a little, waiting for the next plea. It came quickly. "I ain't a murderer, mister. I was only taking orders from Ormsby. If I didn't, I'd have got it myself. A man can't work in this town, or live in this town, without doing what he's told."

"I can't feel sorry for you. Your crowd is framing my friend, Clay Manning. You would have driven me to my death right now, if I hadn't been wise. Sorry, but you'll have to take it."

They passed the gas station, went on another hundred feet. "T-they'll be waiting a half mile down the road," Pond's tortured voice gasped. "They'll riddle me with lead."

"That's right," Ed told him cheerfully.

"S-suppose I talked, mister? S-suppose I cleared your friend, this guy Manning?"

Ed's spine tingled with a thrill of triumph. But he restrained himself, looked ahead along the road, trying not to show his eagerness. "How do I know you can do that? You're only a cab driver. What would *you* know?"

Pond's voice grated harshly. "What would *I* know? I drove this cab out after Manning, when he left the Empire Hotel that day—me and another guy. We watched Manning go into the Pigeon Inn through the back way, an' then we went and 'phoned the State Troopers. It's Flint Ormsby, and his brother, Stan, that's running the gambling racket in this county. Graham, the *Star* reporter, gets the inside dope for them, and they do the shakin' down. Flint Ormsby is dynamite. He likes to do his own killings. It was him that shot Hilda Worth, but I ain't got the proof o' that. But I know Hilda was dead when Clay Manning got there that day! Kedrick wasn't in it at all. Ormsby's pulled the wool over his eyes swell!"

Ed had stopped the car. "You'll write that down for me?"

"I'll write, mister. Yeah. Only don't drive that other half mile!"

Ed nodded. He swung the car around in a complete turn, raced back to the gas station. To the startled attendant, he waved an imperative hand. "Come here and be a witness to this confession!"

He released Pond's arms, thrust paper and fountain-pen at him.

"Write!" he ordered.

Slowly, laboriously, while Ed dangled his .45 suggestively, Pond wrote out everything he had told Ed. The gas station attendant's eyes widened as he read over Pond's shoulder. "Wow! Will this bust the county wide open!"

"That's what Hilda Worth wanted to do," Ed told him dryly.

He was folding the confession, putting it in his pocket, when his eyes narrowed. The black touring sedan had appeared down the road, retracing its course.

Ed Race's eyes glinted. "They're coming back to see what's holding us up," he said. "Well, well. This will be a pleasure!"

He motioned to the attendant. "Get inside. There'll be a lot of shooting here in a minute!"

Pond cowered in the back of the cab, and Ed waited alongside it, on the far side of the cab from the road. There wasn't long to wait.

THE TOURING-SEDAN slowed up, pulling into the driveway. Ormsby stepped out of it, followed by two other men from the rear. They glanced suspiciously about.

Ed stepped out from behind it, took off his chauffeur's cap, and threw it away. He faced the four men, crouching, hands at his sides.

"Here I am, boys," he said mildly.

Ormsby spat out a curse, and his hand darted to his shoulder holster. The other men followed suit.

Ed Race did not seem to have moved. But his hands were suddenly, miraculously, holding two thundering, death-spitting .45 caliber revolvers. That same lightning-fast, eye-defying speed that he demonstrated on the stage, was now being exhibited free, here on the highway. But the men who faced him paid for the exhibition with their lives.

They fired scattered shots, but their slugs went wide, for the twin streams of bullets from Ed's guns mowed them down before they could aim. He shot four times, twice from each gun—and each shot was a bull's-eye, square in the center of a forehead.

The driver of the touring-sedan came leaping out of it with gun in hand, and Ed fired once more. His eyes were cold, bleak, as he stood there spraddle-legged, smoking guns in his hands, and gazed down at the ground, littered with bodies. The gas-station attendant came out. "Lord, what shooting! One against four!"

Ed grinned at him. "Some show, eh? Where's your 'phone?"

He kept his eye on Pond, still cowering in the cab, while he got John Stoneman at the county courthouse. "You can ask for an adjournment till I get back to town. The case is broken," he told the defense attorney. "And you can tell Kedrick for me, that I apologize to him. I thought he was a crook, and I find he was only a prig!"

CORPSE WITHOUT A COFFIN

E D RACE was playing the Glenbold City Theater that week, and had stayed after his number was over, to see the rest of the show. That brought it close to midnight when he started for his hotel. It was pure coincidence that he happened to be passing the corner of Newmarket and South at the moment when the drunken cop stopped the girl in the sedan.

It all happened very fast. Afterward, Ed Race recalled that he had felt scornful when he saw the uniformed policeman step out of Montrose's Bar, and weave toward the curb to cross the street. The man was obviously still on duty, because he carried his nightstick; and he had had much more than he could gracefully hold.

It was just as the cop stepped off the curb that the girl swung her sedan into Newmarket from South Street. Ed, on the opposite side of Newmarket from Montrose's Bar, saw two things, simultaneously. A convertible coupé with a low license number was coming around the corner after the sedan; and the cop was staggering directly into the sedan's path.

The girl swerved sharply to the right to avoid the policeman, but he lurched forward, once more bringing himself into the glare of her headlights. This time the girl could not avoid him. There was a mechanical squeal, and a slithering of rubber tires against cement as she stepped down hard on the brake. Her car rocked to a stop with the front bumper crowding against the cop's shins.

He staggered, clawing at the radiator, and suddenly pulled his hand away as it touched the hot surface. He reached for one of the headlights, steadied himself for a moment, and cursed loudly and indecently. Then he started around to the side of the car, yelling, "So you'll run down a cop, will you? I'll learn you! Let's see your license!"

Ed Race got a glimpse of the girl's face now. It was white, frightened, panicky. But the overwhelming emotions coursing over her features could not obscure their natural beauty. It was a soft, youthful, unspoiled beauty, though now overcast by stark fear. Tousled hair showed over a high forehead, streaking, uncombed, down the nape of her neck. Her throat showed white against the background of some dark garment which she wore, fallen open now, unnoticed, to reveal a curve of small, firm breast.

Ed's interest changed to eager excitement, as he noticed that that garment was not a coat or dress, but a *bathrobe!* The girl's dreadful fear was not warranted by the nature of the incident, and her unconventional attire added to the incongruity of the whole thing.

ED'S EYES swung for an instant to the convertible coupé which had come around the corner behind her. Then he stiffened, his nerves tingling. That coupé had stopped, too, and he could see two men in it. One was leaning over the wheel, watching the scene, while the other's head was bent out the open window. This second man's face was long, gaunt, with a hard, thin mouth. But the thing that quickened Ed Race's pulse was

the sight of a gun barrel poking up just inside the window. The man was not aiming it, apparently did not intend to use it at that precise moment. But the gun was being held ready for something....

A thing like this was right up Ed Race's alley. On the vaude-ville stage, he was an ace headliner, featured under the name of "The Masked Marksman—the Man Who Can Make Guns Talk." His acrobatic juggling act, in which he used hair-trigger .45 caliber revolvers, instead of dumbbells, always received top billing, and his income from his profession was large enough to have satisfied any normal man.

But the nervous energy within him required a stronger outlet than that. He had long ago adopted a sideline—that of criminology. And the two .45's which he always carried in his shoulder holsters had earned him a dreaded reputation in the underworlds of many cities. He held licenses to practice as a private detective in a dozen states, but never accepted a fee for the various services he had rendered in the past. And now he was intensely interested in this frightened girl, who wore only a bathrobe, and in the two armed men so obviously following her.

He started across the street toward her sedan.

The cop was at the girl's window now, bellowing at her. "What kind of a driver do you think you are, anyway? Suppose you'd run me down and killed me?"

Ed was across the street by this time, and close enough to hear her musical contralto voice, low-pitched and well-bred even under the stress of emotion. "But I tried to avoid you, officer. If you hadn't lurched into my path, I would have passed you. And, anyway, I stopped—"

"So it was *my* fault, huh?" snapped the cop. "Well, girlie, you got a nerve. You can tell that to the judge!"

The girl's hand went to her breast in an instinctive gesture of dismay. "You—you're not going to—"

"Yeah, you guessed it!" was the answer. "I'm gonna give you a ticket—reckless driving. Gimme your license!"

The girl began to stammer. "I—I'm sorry, officer, but I left the house in a hurry, and I forgot my bag—"

"So-o!" The cop's tone was laden with vindictive triumph. "You got no license, huh? That's just too bad. You can come to the station house, then!"

Ed was on the other side of the car from the cop. Out of the corner of his eye he saw the two men in the convertible coupé, still watching. But he forgot about them in the excitement of a new discovery. He had approached the sedan from the rear, and now saw what the cop had not yet noticed.

A man's body was curled up on the floor of the sedan behind the girl's seat!

She was talking swiftly now, frantically. "Please, officer, don't stop me now. I—I'll give you my name and address. You can give me a ticket, and I promise to appear. I'm Janet Shelton—Fletcher Shelton's sister."

The cop's intoxicated haze was wearing off a bit, and he paused at mention of the name of Fletcher Shelton, his lips pursing into a nasty leer. "Oh, so you're the sister of that skunk of a reformer that's trying to clean the town up—the way *he* claims. Well, well—that cinches it, girlie. You just come along."

ED RACE had moved around to the cop's side of the car. He had seen that the man curled up in the rear of the car was dead. There was a small black bullet hole, clotted with blood, at the base of his neck. This girl, Janet Shelton, was transporting a murdered man. Whatever her purpose, Ed Race was sure that she was not guilty of murder. Ed was an excellent judge of human nature, and he had often staked his reputation, even his life, on the strength of his own judgment.

Fletcher Shelton's sister was in a spot. She had a murdered man in her car, and was being followed by two armed men. Now the cop was going to pull her in. Ed Race smiled tightly. He had read the local papers of Glenbold City, as he did of every town that he played. He knew that Fletcher Shelton was a starry-eyed reformer whose radio broadcasts had greatly embarrassed the grafting city administration. He knew that Glenbold City was in the hands of an unscrupulous ring of political racketeers who had imported thugs and gunmen and sworn them in as police— of which this cop was a glaring example.

Before he got around alongside that policeman, Ed had decided that the girl needed help—and was going to get it.

He tapped the cop on the shoulder, and said mildly, "Excuse me if I intrude, officer."

Janet Shelton's eyes widened in sudden hope, at his interference, but the look of frightened despair immediately returned.

The cop swung around, glared at Ed. "Huh? Who're you?"

"Just a passer-by," Ed said, still mildly. "I saw the whole incident. I shall be glad to testify—in the young lady's favor!"

The cop's eyebrows lowered, and he stepped closer to Ed. "Is that so!"

"Yes, officer. I shall testify that you were—and are—intoxicated, that you stepped directly in the path of her car. Now—" his tone became soothing—"why don't you forget the whole business? It's obvious that the young lady must have a license to drive a car. It will merely mean that she will have to produce it in court tomorrow. As for the reckless driving charge, that wouldn't hold water, after I testify. Now don't you think it better to drop the whole thing? If you take her in, you'll have to appear in night court, and the judge will certainly notice that you've had a few drinks."

Ed's arguments made no impression on the cop. He snarled,

"Wise guy, huh? You'll testify against me, hey?" He raised his nightstick. "Not with a busted head, you won't testify!"

He started to bring the stick down in a vicious blow. But Ed Race side-stepped nimbly, and smashed a right hook to the cop's jaw. The policeman staggered under the blow, shook his head as if to clear it, and raised the club once more.

Ed's eyes were bleak, his mouth a tight thin line. He drove a hard left to the cop's middle, then brought up a right uppercut, with all the power of his hundred and ninety pounds, to the same spot on the other's jaw. This time Ed wasn't fooling, and there was an ominous crack as his bunched fist crashed home. The cops' head snapped back, and the nightstick flew from nerveless fingers. The man was literally lifted from his feet, and dropped to the ground like an inert meal sack. He was out.

Ed massaged his knuckles, and turned to the girl, smiled at the wide-open stare of her innocent blue eyes. She stammered, "T-thank you. I—I—"

Suddenly her eyes, swinging to the rear-vision mirror, caught sight of something in the street behind her car, and she uttered a startled, "Oh-h!"

ED SWIVLED in that direction, and tautened. The two men had come out of the convertible coupé, and were approaching them. The one from behind the driver's seat was stocky, with a red, almost cherubic face. He carried an automatic, dangling from the forefinger of his right hand, and was grinning. The gaunt man, who had sat beside the driver, was also carrying a gun.

Ed's eyes narrowed, as he faced them.

49

The cherubic man said, "You butt outa this, guy. You stepped into something too big for you. Now be a good boy and scram, before you put your foot in it. We'll take care of the copper. Get it?"

Ed's mild voice was deceptive. "If you gentlemen are detectives. I'm sure I can explain—"

The gaunt, sallow-faced fellow snarled. "You heard him. Scram!"

They still thought he was an ordinary passer-by who had tried to be a Galahad to a lady. Their guns were still hanging lax. They were supremely arrogant, confident that they could master him.

Ed Race acted with all of the lightning speed that had left his audiences stunned in theaters from coast to coast. In those theaters he was accustomed to bringing the house to its feet by doing a back somersault, then flipping a gun out of its holster and shooting out the flame of a candle thirty feet across the stage—almost before his feet touched the ground. Now he gave a similar exhibition—but in deadly earnest.

The girl was leaning from the window of her car, whispering to Ed, "Please, do as they say. You'll only get in trouble. They're killers. They'll kill you, and leave you in the gutter. Please go—"

Ed stopped her. "It's all right, Miss. Don't worry."

His eyes held those two men. They sensed the tautness of his poised body, sensed that they were not to have an easy time with him. The cherubic man, who appeared to be quicker-witted than his gaunt companion, began to raise his gun.

Ed Race's hands leaped up to his shoulder holsters with a

speed that defied the eye. Abruptly, as if by magic, those two heavy .45's were leveled at the two men.

The cherubic one had his gun up, a startled expression on his face as he squeezed the trigger. But Ed's gun barked before the other's. The .45 emitted a deep-throated roar, bucked in Ed's hand, and belched flame. The slug smashed into the cherubic man's shoulder, spinning him around with the force of a sledge-hammer, and deflecting his aim. His bullet went wild, and he fell sideways to the ground, beside the form of the unconscious cop.

The gaunt man snarled, his gun leaping up. Ed's second .45 roared and bucked, and he hit the gaunt man in exactly the same place as he had hit the other. It was cool, perfected shooting. The gaunt man uttered a cry deep in his throat, and staggered backward, holding his shoulder.

Then, from around the corner on South Street, there came the screech of a police car.

ED THOUGHT quickly. There was no use in his running away from this. His bullets were in those two fellows, and the cop could identify him. He had to remain in this town for a week, and he would be sure to be picked up. He might as well stay and face the music. But the girl should go. That dead man in her car was no joke. He turned to tell her to get away. Then a rueful grin twisted his lips. She was gone! He could see the tail-lights of her car turning the far corner, just as the police car swung into Newmarket behind him.

Shrugging, Ed reversed his guns, and handed them to the policeman who sprang from the squad car. "I shot those two mugs," he said. "It was self-defense, as you can see from their guns."

The driver of the squad car came out and stood beside his companion, and they looked down at the wounded men. Then both pursed their lips, and whistled, simultaneously.

"Boy!" said the one who had Ed's guns. "You must be a streak of lightning with a gun. This skinny guy is Sid Gaynor. That's funny, too. Gaynor has killed plenty of men in this town—and it's always self-defense. Now the tables are turned. He's met a guy who can dish it out faster than he can!"

Ed Race asked, "Who's the other?"

Both policemen grew serious. "That one, mister, is the one that's going to be a very swift pain in the neck to you. That is Nick Foldiss!"

"Who's Nick Foldiss?"

The officer laughed. "Stranger in town, eh? Well, in case you really don't know, he's the son of Garth Foldiss. Also, in case you don't know, Garth Foldiss owns this town—*and* runs it."

Ed said quietly, "Looks bad for me, eh?"

The cop whom he had knocked out had begun to stir, and now he sat up, holding his jaw. "It looks worse than that for you, guy! Assaulting an officer, too. Take him in, Spurgeon," he said to the officer from the squad car," and watch him. He's dangerous!"

THE VARIED crowd of shyster lawyers, bail bondsmen, runners, and morbid curiosity seekers, who infest the night courts of every city, filled the benches of the Newbold City night court. They stirred with interest as Judge Frazer rapped his gavel and said, "Next case!"

The clerk picked up a complaint form from the top of the pile on his desk and called out, "Number One-thousand-seven-en-hundred sixty-three. People against Ed Race. Complaint, City Patrolman Felix Nedeen, Badge Number Ninety-seven."

The grilled door at the right of the courtroom opened, and Patrolman Felix Nedeen entered, with his hand on Ed Race's shoulder. Nedeen was holding a wet compress to his jaw where Ed had smashed him, and casting venomous glances at Ed. He led his prisoner in front of the bench, and a young deputy assistant district attorney stepped forward to glance at the complaint.

Judge Frazer looked quizzically at Ed, sizing up his five-foot-eight of supple litheness, his keen eyes, and the touch of a smile on his lips. He frowned. "What's the charge here?"

The young D.A. read the complaint, "Resisting an officer in the performance of his duties; assaulting an officer; carrying concealed weapons; assault with deadly weapons, with intent to kill."

The judge said, "Hm, there are still a few more sections of the Criminal Code that you haven't broken, young man. How do you plead?"

The D.A. interrupted. "Excuse me, Your Honor. I notice that the two last charges—carrying concealed weapons, and assault with intent to kill—have been stricken out. There's a note here from the complaint clerk that the two men, who were shot by this defendant, have made a statement in the hospital that it was a mistake, that they thought he was a holdup man and fired at him first. They do not wish to make any charges against him."

Ed Races' eyes narrowed, as he heard this. As he had figured the set-up, Nick Foldiss and Sid Gaynor, the two gunmen, must have been following the girl in the interests of Garth Foldiss, the boss of the city. In that event, what could have been simpler than to throw the book at Ed Race, send him to trial on every charge they could work up? There was something wrong here. He said nothing, listening to the D.A. continue.

"As for the charge of carrying concealed weapons, it now appears that the defendant has a private detective's license to operate in the state, and also a permit to carry a gun. Therefore, the only charges remaining are those preferred by Patrolman Nedeen here, who claims to have been assaulted by the defendant."

The D.A. was a young man of perhaps twenty-seven, with close-cropped black hair, and small, shrewd eyes. He looked to Ed to be the type of young politician who has obtained his job by hanging around political clubs and currying the favor of the boss. In that case, he would be working for the boss. Ed had shot Nick Foldiss, the boss's son. And he couldn't understand why they were so easy with him, why the D.A. was actually speaking almost sneeringly of the assault charge preferred by Nedeen.

Judge Frazer glanced at the patrolman. "You claim that this defendant attacked you while you were attempting to make an arrest?"

Nedeen nodded. The liquor had worn off by this time, leaving him mean and ugly. "Yes, Your Honor. This girl in the sedan almost ran me down, and she didn't have no license. I was going to take her in, when this man interfered—"

He stopped, trailing off uncertainly, as he saw that the judge was not listening to him, but was looking down toward the door at the other end of the courtroom.

Ed looked too, and became more and more puzzled. A murmur went up from the crowd in the seats. Ed could hear the whispers, "It's Garth Foldiss, himself!"

THE MAN who had entered was huge. He must have been all of six feet, and thick in the waist, with a red, animal-strong face. Deep, intense eyes stared out from under heavy-bushed brows. It was easy for Ed to see how Garth Foldiss had been able to make himself the political boss of Glenbold City. Given time, there was no question but what the man could extend his power to embrace the state.

The judge wavered a moment, apparently waiting to see what Garth Foldiss would do. The boss came slowly down the aisle, his eyes fixed upon Ed, studying him.

Ed had half-turned to face him, and he thought that it was too bad for that girl, Janet Shelton, if she was attempting to pit her feeble innocence against the stark ruthlessness that shone in Garth Foldiss's eyes. That was no job for a woman to try.

Foldiss came up alongside Ed, facing the bench. "If it please the court," he said in his deep booming voice, "I understand that this defendant is charged with resisting an officer in the performance of his duty—namely, the arrest of a young lady who this officer claims almost ran him down?"

Judge Frazer asked hesitantly, almost timidly, "What is your interest in this case, Mr. Foldiss?"

Foldiss laughed deep in his chest. "My son and another man were shot by this defendant in a mistaken argument. I understand that Officer Nedeen here states that there was a young lady whom he attempted to arrest. I appear here merely as an *amicus curiae*—a friend of the court—in the interests of justice. I do not wish to see this defendant punished for something that was not his fault. If I may have five minutes alone with the defendant and the complaining officer, I think I can straighten out the whole situation."

The judge nodded reluctantly. It was apparent that he did not relish Foldiss's overbearing manner, nor his attempt to run the court in this way. But there was little that he could do. Foldiss controlled the city council, and the mayor's office, and there had been instances where judges who had not toed the mark had found themselves facing impeachment proceedings. Everybody knew that Foldiss was in the habit of striding up and down the aisles of the city council room, ordering the city councilors how to vote. It would be simple for him to trump up some charge against Judge Frazer, and force through impeachment proceedings.

The judge said, "Very well. You may talk to the defendant and the complaining officer. I will call the case again in five minutes." **FOLDISS GRINNED,** and took Ed Race by the arm, led him to a corner, out of earshot of the court clerk. He motioned to Officer Nedeen to wait. Ed faced him coldly, waiting.

"You're Ed Race, the Masked Marksman—the one who's appearing at the Glenbold Theater, aren't you?" Foldiss began.

Ed nodded. "That's right." He hid the puzzlement in his eyes. It was apparent that Foldiss wanted something from him.

"Okay. You shot my son, Nick; but he tells me it was a mistake."

"It wasn't a mistake," Ed told him. "Your son and that gunman with him knew I wasn't a hold-up man. They wanted to get to the girl—Miss Shelton. I wouldn't let them."

Foldiss brows contracted. "Now look here, Race, don't make it hard for yourself. I can *get* you out of this jam. But I can also sink you in so deep you'll rot in jail. Take your choice."

Ed considered him a moment. "What do you want me to do?"

Foldiss's lips wreathed in a smile. "That's better. What I want you to do is fair enough. You just take a plea of guilty to simple assault against this cop, and I'll get the judge to give you a suspended sentence. You can walk out of here a free man."

Ed Race grinned thinly. "No thanks, Mr. Foldiss. I'm not having any, thank you."

Foldiss glowered at him. "I'm willing to give you a break. You could get a year for resisting an officer; and you could get two years for attacking an officer. If you stay stubborn, I'll see that Frazer gives you the limit."

"That's fine, Mr. Foldiss," Ed said. "And you could also have your son and his friend, Sid Gaynor, come over here and sign the complaint for the other two charges. That would add another five years, wouldn't it?" He smiled sourly.

Foldiss gazed at him intently, chewing his lower lip. "Now look here, Race, why not be reasonable? You're only piling up trouble for yourself this way."

"I don't think so," Ed said.

"What do you mean?"

"I mean that for some reason, you don't want any mention made in court, of the girl, Janet Shelton—or of what she was carrying in that car of hers," said Ed "I'm thinking that you'll get me out of this without my having to plead guilty."

Foldiss' face had frozen into a noncommittal mask as Ed spoke. He whistled, very low. "*So-o*—you know all about that? And I thought from what Nick and Sid Gaynor told me, that you were just a passer-by that got mixed into the thing!" He lowered his voice. "What's your game, Race? Are you out to buck me?"

Ed shrugged. "No game, Foldiss. And I don't like you or your dirty crew. I'm going to enter a plea of 'not guilty.' I'm going to hire the best lawyers in the state to handle this case. I'm going to get to the bottom of it."

The big, red-faced political boss seemed about to have a stroke. He spluttered, half raised a fist as if to strike Ed, then thought better of it. He swung abruptly away from Ed, and went over to Officer Felix Nedeen, buttonholed him in a corner, and talked confidentially in a low voice. Nedeen listened, at first sullenly, then with a sudden, bright, malicious glow in his mean eyes. At last, he nodded eagerly.

Foldiss smiled, and looked up toward the door at the far end of the courtroom. A thin little runt of a man, with big ears and an oversized coat, was standing out there. Foldiss nodded to this man, almost imperceptibly, and the man smirked, turned and hurried out.

Now Foldiss led Officer Nedeen to the bench, and waited till the current case had been disposed of. Then he said, "Your

Honor, Officer Nedeen has a statement to make in the matter of the case of the People against Ed Race." He walked around beside the bench, and motioned to the young D.A., who also approached.

The three of them whispered for several moments, and then Judge Frazer shrugged. "All right, Mr. Foldiss, but it doesn't look right—"

Foldiss laughed his booming laugh. "Don't worry, Judge." He stepped back, and took a seat in the first row of chairs. The D.A. motioned Nedeen and Ed Race before the judge, and Frazer said, "All right, officer. You have a statement to make?"

Nedeen looked viciously at Ed, and began to talk in a low voice. "I wish to withdraw the complaint against this defendant, as I believe that any blow he may have struck was done by accident. Since Mr. Race is a well-known vaudeville actor, and holds a private detective's license, I do not wish to embarrass him. I therefore wish to withdraw the complaint."

Nedeen's words were certainly friendly enough, but there was a little triumphant smirk around the corners of his lips, and a sardonic gleam in his eyes, that Ed did not like. He was startled at Nedeen's sudden change of front, and he suspected that something sinister lay behind it. But he could not very well insist on being held.

Judge Frazer said shortly, "In view of the withdrawal of this complaint, and with the consent of the district attorney, I discharge the defendant. You may go, Mr. Race!"

Ed smiled. "Thank you, sir," he said. Then to Nedeen, "May I have my guns back, please?"

Nedeen started. "Your—guns?" He seemed puzzled as to what to do, and his glance went to Foldiss, still seated among the spectators, as if for guidance.

Foldiss sprang up, whispered in Nedeen's ear, and the policeman grinned. "Sure, Mr. Race. Just a minute. I'll get 'em for you."

Ed stepped aside to make room for the next case, and Nedeen went into the complaint-room, came out after a minute or two with the two well polished .45's. Ed took them from him, and spun the barrels from force of habit, as he slipped them back into the shoulder holsters. Suddenly a tingle went up Ed's spine. His practiced fingers had detected that the barrels spun too easily. The weight of the cartridges was lacking from them.

Nedeen had unloaded both guns before giving them to him!

ED ALLOWED no trace of the discovery to show in his face. The motion of holstering the guns was completed smoothly, and he nodded to the young D.A., glanced carelessly at Foldiss, who had seated himself as if to watch the further court proceedings.

Ed's lips quirked in a humorous smile. He turned to the complaining cop. "Come on, Nedeen. No hard feelings. I'll buy you a drink."

Nedeen started to walk down the aisle with him out of force of habit. "That's okay, Race." Then suddenly something seemed to occur to him, and he started to draw away. "Never mind, Race. Skip it. I'll be seeing you. I gotta go back in the complaint-room—"

Ed gripped his arm, walking close to him. "Oh, come on. You know you like a drink—and you're off duty now."

Nedeen was embarrassed by the eyes of the spectators upon

them as they walked up the aisle. He tried to pull away, but Ed held him closely, propelling him toward the door. They were out of the courtroom now, in the foyer. The broad double-doors leading to the street were facing them, and Ed could see a car pulled out outside, directly opposite the entrance. It seemed to be waiting.

He kept his grip on Nedeen fairly dragging him toward that door. Nedeen's face grew white. "Nix, Race. Go ahead. I gotta stay—"

"I wouldn't think of it," Ed protested.

They were outside now, and Nedeen was struggling almost frantically.

Ed Race was laughing grimly. There were three men in the car across the street, and the barrel of a sub-machine gun was poking out of the rear window, pointing at them. Ed had known that something like this was scheduled to happen, when he found that his guns were unloaded. He had extra cartridges in his pocket, and could have loaded them before coming out. But he had seen the holstered service revolver in Nedeen's Sam Browne belt, and he had figured that it would do just as well. But he had not counted on a sub-machine gun.

Now the wicked-looking snout of the weapon was all the way out of the window, and Ed could distinguish, behind it, the pinched features of the little man with the big ears, to whom Foldiss had signaled, inside the courtroom.

That man had orders to cut down Ed Race, and he wasn't going to stop merely because a policeman was with him!

Nedeen realized what was going to happen. He uttered a

61

choked cry, and tried desperately to pull away. But Ed's muscular fingers tightened on his arm, swung him around for a shield. At the same time, Ed yanked the service revolver from Nedeen's holster.

It was at that instant that the submachine gun began to chatter. Simultaneously, with the deadly staccato rattle of the tommy-gun, a girl's scream sounded, shrill and clear from down the street.

That scream only registered subconsciously with Ed Race, for his every faculty was focused upon the business in hand. What he did, in the next split-second, was what he was used to doing daily on the stage, for the benefit of a paying audience. However, when he had done it on the stage, a false move or misstep would have resulted only in the spoiling of the act. Now, the slightest mistake meant death.

That machine gun was stuttering, sending a creeping hail of splattering lead against the steps of the court—a hail that moved swiftly upward to where it would smash into the bodies of Ed Race and Patrolman Nedeen.

Ed had Nedeen's service revolver in his hand. He straight-armed the patrolman, so that Nedeen went toppling backward off the steps to one side, and out of the path of the machine-gun swath. Ed, himself, leaped in the other direction, landing lithely on his feet on the right-hand side of the steps. As he landed, he snapped a single shot at the face of the big-eared man behind the tommy-gun.

That face seemed suddenly to explode, as Ed's slug smashed it. The marching lead from the muzzle of the sub-machine gun wavered, trickled off into nothingness, and the silence was abruptly oppressive.

Two swift revolver shots came from the second of the three men in the car, both clanging ineffectually into the masonry of the courthouse. Ed fired again, at the flashes, and scored a hit. A man's quick scream sounded, swiftly choking to a gurgle. Then the driver of the death-car gave up. He clashed gears in his panicky, frightened hurry to get away from that deadly accurate shooting of Ed Race's. The sedan lurched away, sped down the street.

In the courthouse there was a frenzy of pandemonium. White faces peered out, but no one ventured into the street.

ED SAW a second car swinging down toward him, and instinctively raised his gun. But he lowered it at once when he saw that the girl, Janet Shelton, was behind the wheel. She was still in her bathrobe, her hair disarranged, but she looked sweet, innocent and frightened.

She motioned urgently to Ed, who ran across to the curb and leaped on the running board. She threw him a quick half-smile.

Ed glanced hastily into the rear of the car. The body of the murdered man was gone. She must have disposed of it, somehow.

She said swiftly, "I had to come back and see what they did to you. I saw Crumpit and those others waiting in the car, but I thought they were only going to follow you. I didn't think they meant to get rid of you *that* way, too!"

She was racing the car on, as she spoke, and Ed, glancing behind, saw that Officer Nedeen lay on the pavement where he had pushed him. Nedeen was on hands and knees, watching them, uncertainly. Ed had saved his life, but he was sure that Nedeen would have shot him then, if he'd had a gun.

In the doorway of the courthouse, a crowd was surging out; the giant figure of Garth Foldiss was in the lead. Foldiss raised his gun at Ed.

Ed merely lifted Nedeen's service .38, hanging on to the careening car with one hand. Garth Foldiss hastily leaped backward into the crowd behind him, without firing. Ed grinned, and turned to see where the girl was heading.

She swung around the corner on two wheels, and Ed hung on, grimly. Ahead, he could now see the tail-lights of the fleeing car which had attacked him at the courthouse. He bent low, so that his head was on a level with the window.

"Follow that sedan," he told the girl. "But stay behind, so he won't notice us."

The girl nodded, facing forward. "Are you all right out there?"

Ed laughed harshly. "Don't worry about me—I can hang on. I've been in plenty tougher spots!" He looked at her.

"And all because of me!" the girl exclaimed, expertly veering the car into Glenbold Boulevard after the fleeing sedan. It was almost three o'clock in the morning, and the traffic lights weren't working any more. The car ahead was picking up speed, increasing the distance between them. But the boulevard was wide, straight as an arrow, and it was easy to keep the sedan in sight.

The girl increased their speed.

Ed bent down again, asked, "Where did you get rid of the— er—body? There *was* a body, wasn't there?"

Janet Shelton started, perceptibly. Her hands wavered on the wheel, and the car swerved, but she got it under control again, keeping her eyes on the tail-lights ahead.

"You saw that body—and yet you helped me? I might have been the one who murdered him. You might have been compounding a murder by helping me get away from that drunken policeman!"

Ed laughed. "Not you, Miss Shelton. I'm a pretty good judge of human nature. You didn't murder anybody!"

"Who—who are you?"

For answer, Ed pointed to the marquee of the Glenbold Theater, which they were passing. "That's me—the name on the top line."

The girl's eyes flicked over to the marquee, read the electric-light letters, now dark, but legible in the light of a street-lamp—

THE MASKED MARKSMAN
THE MAN WHO CAN MAKE GUNS TALK!

THE COLD winter wind was whistling past, cutting against Ed's face as he hung on to the speeding car. But he didn't mind. He was oblivious of it as the girl, staring straight ahead after the car she was following, began to talk, speaking loudly enough to be heard by Ed, out on the running-board.

"My brother, Fletcher Shelton, is fighting the crooked politicians in this city, tooth and nail," she said. "Garth Foldiss has been out to get him for a long time. Tonight Foldiss played his trump card. When I got home, I found the body of that dead man in my brother's den. He was just a nobody, a little book-maker, working for Garth Foldiss. But they had shot him with my brother's gun. Then they struck my brother on the head, leaving him there, unconscious, to be found next to the body." The girl paused, breathing agitatedly.

"When I found them all there, I was panic-stricken. It looked just as if Fletcher had really shot this man, and then fallen against his own desk in the struggle, striking his head against a corner. They wouldn't have dared to kill my brother outright, because he has too large a following in Glenbold now, and such a murder would have aroused public sentiment. But, this way, they had him framed perfectly. They could try him in their own courts, railroading him for murder."

She paused, paying attention to the wheel, as the car ahead turned right off Glenbold Boulevard, and headed north, along the Waterford Turnpike.

Ed said, "Stop a minute." She pulled up, and he ran around, got into the seat behind her. "Go ahead," he ordered. "You can stay far behind now. We won't lose him on this road."

She nodded, got the car going again, and Ed set about loading his two .45's.

"There isn't much more to tell," the girl went on. "I was panic-stricken when I saw Fletcher lying beside the dead man. All I could think of was that the police would be coming soon, and Garth Foldiss's scheme would work. I tried to revive Fletcher. He opened his eyes, but was groggy, and still only semi-conscious. The only thing I could think of was to remove that body. It hadn't bled much, and I forced myself to carry it out into my car. Just as I got the body in, I heard a police car coming. I started to drive away, and Nick Foldiss, in that convertible coupé, came along. He and Gaynor must have recognized me, guessed what I was doing. They followed me. You know the rest."

Ed nodded. "Poor kid. You're bucking a tough outfit here. What did you finally do with the body?"

"I drove away, as you were shooting down Foldiss and Gaynor," said the girl. "I drove out toward Waterford, where Fletcher and I have a summer cottage. I put the body in that cottage, then went out and 'phoned Fletcher. The police had gone, only finding Fletcher at the house, and not the murdered man. Fletcher was better by this time, and I told him what I'd done with the dead body. He said he'd attend to it, and I got back in the car and drove to night court to see what would happen to you."

Ed was silent a while, as they drove out on the Waterford Turnpike, following the sedan of the gunmen. Then he said, "You should know, of course, that your 'phone must have been tapped, if you're up against a crowd like Foldiss's. That means that you were overheard when you told your brother Fletcher what you'd done with the dead body."

Janet Shelton gasped. "I hadn't thought of that! Then they *must* know—"

"Certainly. Where did you say this cottage was?"

"Near Waterford...." Her voice slowly trailed off as she realized that they were on the Waterford Turnpike now—that car ahead was racing toward Waterford.

"That's right," Ed said in reply to her unspoken thought.

"They've probably found the place already. They probably rigged a trap, and lay in wait for your brother to get there. It would make no difference to them if he were arrested for the murder at your home, or at the cottage."

A little moan escaped from Janet Shelton's throat. "Then—then all my work was for nothing. That gruesome work of carrying the body, driving with it in the car...." Her knuckles were white against the wheel. "What will I do? They'll be merciless with Fletcher—"

"I'll tell you what we're going to try!" Ed said, coming to a quick decision. "There's no time to explain. Just do as I say. Speed up, and catch that sedan!"

SHE OBEYED him unquestioningly. Her speedometer flew around the dial from sixty to seventy, to seventy-five, until the needle hovered around eighty.

The gunman in the car ahead must have been in a state of nervous funk. With his two dead accomplices in the sedan, he hadn't paid much attention to the back road. Now Ed saw him pick up speed as their two powerful headlights crept up on him. But it was too late. They were almost abreast of him.

Ed cried, "Pass him, and force him toward the ditch. Try to make him stop. Think you can do it?"

Janet Shelton's lips were pressed hard together. "I can do anything now!" she managed to gasp, and swung past the sedan, pulling the wheel over sharply toward the right.

There was a squeal of brakes from the other car, and the gunman driver swung almost toward the ditch to avoid her. Ed

Race was out of the sedan almost before it had stopped, poking the .38 against the gunman's cheek.

"Take it easy now, and come out of there," he ordered.

The gunman had no fight in him. He had not even attempted to use his own gun, which had been kept handily on the seat next to him. The bloody bodies of the machine-gunner and his mate, in the rear of the car, still lay there to testify to the deadliness of Ed Race's shooting, and this fellow had no stomach to trade lead with Ed.

He stepped out of the car, his hands high in the air.

Janet Shelton came around beside Ed, and stared at the prisoner.

"Glone!" she exclaimed. "You—you...." Her voice choked upon itself in indignation.

The gunman, Glone, lowered his eyes before hers.

Janet turned to Ed. "This man was working for my brother as an investigator, taking his pay. And now he turns up driving a murder-car for Garth Foldiss! He—he's betrayed Fletcher!"

Ed Race said softly, "A rat, eh?"

Glone lifted his glance, met the cold contempt in Ed's eyes. Something there frightened him. He stammered, "I—I couldn't help it, mister. There's no use bucking Garth Foldiss's outfit. I wouldn't of lasted a day."

"That's too bad," Ed said softly. "Because you're not going to last any longer this way." He raised the .38. "I'm going to give you what a rat deserves!"

Glone shrieked, *"No! God, no!"*

Janet Shelton exclaimed, "You're not going to—"

Ed Race nodded inexorably. He was bluffing. He had never killed a man in cold blood in his life. But Glone could not tell that he was bluffing. The wretched gunman saw only the cold, steely glint in Ed's eyes, the hard line of his lips.

Glone screamed, "No, no, mister. Hold it! I can tell you plenty. I'll spill the works." His voice shrilled in a desperate effort to head off the tightening trigger finger of Ed's right hand. "I saw the guy bumped in Shelton's house. I can tell you who did it. I can lay it on the line for you! Please give me a chance!"

Ed sighed imperceptibly. He had been afraid that he would have to back down on his bluff. "Who murdered that man?" he asked hoarsely.

"Garth Foldiss did it himself," cried Glone. "I let him in the house. I went there to make a phony report to Fletcher Shelton, and I let Garth in, the back way, with this bookie. Foldiss wanted to knock the bookie off anyway, for a double-cross. He figured it would be a swell stunt to lay it on to Shelton. While I was talking to Shelton, Foldiss came in and smacked him on the head, then called in the bookie, and shot him in the back of the head. Then we both scrammed—"

Ed's eyes were gleaming with triumph. He pulled out a small notebook, and a fountain-pen, thrust them at Glone. "Write that all down!" he ordered.

Glone wrote.

He had just finished signing his name when a pair of powerful headlights came blasting down at them from the direction of Glenbold City. A car screamed to a stop alongside, and Garth Foldiss, with two men piled out. He pointed at Ed.

"Burn him down!"

THE TWO men had naked guns. They were shooting almost as they came out of the car. The bark of Ed's .38 mingled with the roar of their guns. The night was split by deafening detonations. Ed was shooting coolly, carefully, accurately. The two men were shooting fast, hoping to accomplish with a hail of lead what they might not be able to do with careful sharpshooting. Their slugs smashed into the car in a vicious staccato tattoo.

Ed thrust Janet Shelton out of the way, as he fired. A scream sounded from Glone, beside him, but Ed wasn't looking. He was squinting into the hail of lead, firing at the faces behind those barking guns. He saw the two gunmen go down with holes drilled accurately in the center of their foreheads, each the replica of the other.

Now he swung the .38 toward Garth Foldiss, who had stepped behind his car for protection. Foldiss was peering out from the back, gun in hand, looking for an opportunity to shoot.

Ed laughed tauntingly. "Got to do your own shooting now, Foldiss—but not in the back. Come on out!"

Foldiss didn't come out. He fired hastily, and pulled his head back. The shot went wild, and Ed pulled the trigger of the .38. There was only an empty click.

Suddenly, wild, triumphant laughter burst from Garth Foldiss. "Your gun's empty, Race! That's Nedeen's gun. And your own, 45's are empty. I told Nedeen to unload them before he gave them to you! I'm coming out now, Race. I'm going to shoot you down like a dog—and that Shelton girl, too! Then I'm going to the cottage, and notify the cops. They'll come and find Fletcher Shelton with the murdered bookie. It's all worked out, anyway!"

Garth Foldiss came stalking out from behind the car, supremely confident, the gun dangling from his hand. He was enjoying this a lot. His lips curled in a sneer. "Can you take it, Race?"

Janet Shelton uttered a whimpering cry, raised a hand to her breast. Her bathrobe had fallen open in front again, but she forgot everything in the sudden thought that this man, who had tried so hard to help her, was going to die without a chance.

Garth Foldiss advanced slowly, trying to prolong the moment of vindictive triumph. "Well Race—*can you take it?*"

"Yes," Ed said mildly. *"But can you?"*

And suddenly his lithe body snapped into electrifying action. He bent at the knees, swerved, and threw himself into a back-somersault like the ones he did on the stage every day. Ed flipped away from where Janet Shelton was standing, and Garth Foldiss raised his gun, eyes narrowing in bewilderment at the swiftly moving lines of Ed's somersaulting body. He tried to aim the gun, pressing the trigger. But he never had a chance to fire.

For Ed Race's two forty-fives were out in his hands, and he was shooting even as he rolled—just as he did on the stage. On the stage, he had to put out the flames of a row of candles thirty feet away while he did his back-somersault. This was much easier. A man's body is easier to hit than a candle.

Garth Foldiss uttered a long, piercing shriek, and went down with two heavy, smashing .45 caliber slugs in his heart. The shriek died in his throat, his feet kicked convulsively—and he was dead.

ED RACE got up from the ground, holstered his guns, dusted himself off, and grinned at Janet Shelton. He stepped over to where the gunman, Glone, lay with his head against the car. The first fusillade had got him. He had just signed the confession in time.

Ed stepped over to Janet Shelton and put an arm around her shoulders. She was shivering. He gently wrapped her bathrobe around her, and helped her to her car. "We'll leave this carrion here for a while. With this confession of Glone's—" he took the notebook from her trembling fingers—"we shouldn't have any difficulty in clearing your brother."

She stopped shivering. In the car she looked up at him. A tender smile played at her lips. "I—I must come and see you in the theater sometime," she said. "Your act must be very good."

"Do that," Ed told her. "I'll send you a couple of passes."

Suddenly she cried—happily.

Ed Race drove through the night, smiling.

THE CORPSE TAKES A
CURTAIN CALL

THE DOORMAN at the Clareton Hotel greeted Ed Race warmly, as an old patron. Ed let him take his bags out of the cab, paid off the driver and turned to enter the hotel. Then abruptly he stopped, body tautening, lips thinning into a tight line. The long powerful fingers of his right hand hovered up near his necktie where they would be within swift reach of one of the two heavy .45's which he carried in twin shoulder holsters.

His narrowed eyes met the faintly mocking gaze of Duke Sundelius, who was just emerging from the Clareton, followed by "Sonny" Conwell, his bodyguard.

Sundelius threw a quick order over his shoulder at Conwell. "Take it easy, Sonny!" Then he faced Ed Race and said banteringly, "Too bad you had to come back to New York, Race. The air in Florida is much healthier for you right now."

Sundelius had a thin face in which were set a pair of high narrow eyes that almost never blinked. Men swore they had watched Sundelius over the baccarat table at the Sundelius Club, and that the man had sat there for hours without blinking. Men told many other stories about Sundelius, but most of them were in whispers.

Ed Race met the gambler's gaze, and said steadily, "You know why I came back, Sundelius. I'm going to testify at Sonny's trial tomorrow. I'm going to testify before a jury, that I saw Sonny

The muzzle caught him on the chin.

run down Julius Opperman that day, and that it wasn't an accident—but was *deliberate!*"

Ed swung his eyes to meet the cold glare of Sonny Conwell, who had moved up alongside of Duke Sundelius. "Your boss was pretty smart, Sonny, to get the charge against you reduced to manslaughter, so you could get out on bail. If you'd take my advice, though, you'd lam. Because when I finish testifying tomorrow, you'll fry!"

Sonny Conwell uttered an obscene snarl, and started his hand toward his shoulder. But Sundelius' sharp voice stopped him. "Lay off, you fool! Do you think you can beat Race with a gun?"

Conwell grunted, and lowered his hand. His eyes still locked with Ed's. "I'd like to smack a hunk of lead through that mouth of yours!" he spat out. "Why don't you mind your own business? Who asked you to tell the cops what you saw? I thought you was a right guy!"

Ed said tightly, "That was murder, Conwell. Opperman tried to dodge you, and you swerved so as to hit him. You stepped on the gas instead of braking. Opperman was no criminal. He was only a poor fool who lost a lot of money at your boss's club, and couldn't pay up. It's always been Sundelius' way to do his killings openly, but in such a way that they couldn't be called murder. Well, this is one time when your boss and you slipped. I saw it, and I'm not afraid to talk. I'm going to see that you get the chair tomorrow, and I hope you talk before they give you the juice, and incriminate your boss!"

Conwell choked back an oath, and Sundelius smiled grimly. "Don't be too sure of yourself, Race. The trial isn't till tomorrow. *I hope you stay healthy till then!*"

He jerked his head at Conwell, and the two of them strode west toward Broadway.

Ed heard the taxi driver behind him expel a long breath. "Gosh, mister, you sure tangled with a tough one. I thought for a minute they was going to start blasting—and me right behind you!"

"I wish they *had* started blasting!" Ed said grimly. He strode across toward the hotel, and passed through the revolving door into the lobby.

HIS EYES had become speculative. Duke Sundelius hadn't been here at the Clareton by accident, just at the time of Ed's arrival. There must be a deep and calculated reason for it. Sundelius wouldn't be fool enough to appear here if he had planned to have one of his gunmen make an attempt on Ed's life. Besides that wasn't the Duke's way. There was no doubt that he was planning some deadly sort of trick to prevent Ed Race from testifying tomorrow—but it would take a more subtle form than the coarse shootings of the average gangster. Duke's methods had always been the envy of the underworld. And Duke Sundelius had his back to the wall now, for he knew that Sonny Conwell would certainly talk if he went to the electric chair.

Absently, Ed picked up the pen and signed the register at the desk. The clerk said, "Your room is reserved for you, Mr. Race. Eleven-seventeen—the same you had last time."

Ed thanked him, and turned away to find dour old Inspector MacSpain at his elbow.

MacSpain was a good deal past fifty, but there was no fat on him, and he was almost as tall as Ed. His pearl-gray fedora did not conceal the whiteness of his hair. But his cheeks were ruddy, his mouth and chin firm, and there was a steely glint in his eyes which showed he had lost none of the deadly efficiency which had brought him his present job.

He smiled bleakly, and said, "How are you, Ed? I've been waiting for you. I want to make sure nothing happens to you between tonight and tomorrow."

Ed grinned. "It's refreshing to have a cold-blooded eel like you worried about my health, Mac."

MacSpain took his arm. "I'd be worried even if you weren't the star witness at Conwell's trial, Ed. I've known you since the day when I got the Broadway assignment as a first-grade detective. You've done me real favors more than once. In a way, I'm sorry that it has to be you that gets Sundelius down on him."

Ed Race shrugged. "Don't feel too bad about it, Mac. I've been able to take care of myself for a long time now."

"I know that—and Sundelius knows it too. That's why I'm afraid he'll rig some special and infernal trick up for you," MacSpain agreed. "I'm going up to your room with you, Ed. I'll stick with you all evening—that is, if you don't mind my company."

"You won't be much company," Ed told him sourly, "if you're on duty. I want a couple of drinks."

MacSpain smiled. "I'm officially off duty tonight. This is on my own time."

"Good!" Ed exclaimed. "I'll go up, take a shower and change, and then we'll go down to the bar. What do you say?"

"Right. But I'm going up with you while you do it." MacSpain's visage suddenly became grim. "Ed, it's the first chance in ten years that I've had of getting the goods on Sundelius. That man has killed indiscriminately, and he's terrorized people and flouted the law." The inspector's eyes were hard and bleak. "I don't want to miss up this time. If Sonny Conwell is convicted of murder, he'll open up—then we'll have a chance to rid the town of the crookedest, rottenest gambler we've ever had!"

Ed Race nodded sympathetically. He knew that Inspector MacSpain was one of those policemen who took their jobs with the utmost seriousness, wholeheartedly devoted to the performance of duty. He also agreed with MacSpain that the city needed to be rid of Sundelius.

They started toward the elevator together, and just then a bell-hop came through the lobby calling, "Telephone for Inspector MacSpain! Inspector MacSpain!"

The inspector frowned. "I'll get that down here, Ed. Meet you in your room—eleven seventeen, isn't it? Be careful—watch yourself till I get up."

ED GOT in the elevator with the bellboy who was carrying his luggage, and they rode to the eleventh floor. His room, which he usually occupied when in New York, faced southwest with a view of the entire Empire State building and of the upper bay, as well as of the Jersey shore across the river. It was fairly large, with private bath and shower, and Ed got a special rate on it because he was in the theatrical game.

On the vaudeville stage, Ed Race was one of the headline numbers of the Partages Circuit. He appeared as "The Masked Marksman—the Man who can Make Guns Talk." His act consisted of a series of almost miraculous juggling acts; with this difference from the usual act of that kind—he used six heavy .45 caliber hair-trigger revolvers instead of dumb-bells. In juggling those guns, he performed feats of marksmanship which invariably left his audience breathless. The finale, which always evoked thunderous applause, was a routine wherein he did a back somersault while all the guns were in the air—then, catching them as they came down, he fired each in turn, extinguishing the flames of a row of candles thirty feet across the stage.

It had come to be an aphorism on Broadway, that when Ed Race missed one of those candles the end of the world would arrive. Carnarvon, the well-known betting commissioner had turned down odds of fifteen to one that Ed would miss on any given night.

But all this was Ed Race's business. He was used to the applause and to the extremely large salary he drew each week from the Partages Circuit. His nervous energy craved some other outlet besides that of the stage, and he had chosen an avocation which gave him that outlet—the avocation of criminology. He dabbled in crime as other men played the races or collected stamps. He held licenses to operate as a private detective in a dozen states, and the underworld had just cause to fear him and the two .45's that he always carried.

Many attempts had been made upon his life in the past, and he expected that there would be other attempts in the future. But he knew very well that at this time he had never had a more deadly enemy than Duke Sundelius.

Now he was careful to throw his quick glance over every part of the room as he entered it with the bellhop. The boy opened a window, and Ed gave him his tip.

"Who has the room next to this?" he asked.

"It's a guy I took up, sir," the boy told him. "A young fellow named Linton—Frank Linton. That's all I know about him, sir, except that he's had a couple of men call to see him today. I brought drinks up twice."

Ed nodded, and the bellboy left. Ed stood for a moment, inspecting the room. The door of the bathroom was partly open, and he could see into it. He removed his coat, put it in the closet, and started to take off the harness of his two shoulder holsters, with their heavy revolvers.

Then he stopped, taut, every nerve alert. He had distinctly caught a low sound from the bathroom.

Carefully, making no noise on the thick rug, he moved over alongside the bathroom door. Effortlessly, without even thinking, one of the .45's came into his hand.

He remembered clearly that he had looked into the bathroom, and had seen no one there. His mind ran swiftly over the picture of the bathroom, and suddenly he smiled tightly. For he recalled that the shower sheet had been drawn across the front of the stand-up shower. Someone was behind that sheet!

If Sundelius had planted some one there to kill him, it was a crude thing to do. The killer would find it hard to escape from the hotel—especially with Mac-Spain on the way up.

MacSpain! Something clicked in Race's brain. That telephone call in the lobby had been timed too perfectly to be a coincidence—just the right moment to keep the inspector from coming up with him. The whole thing began to have the earmarks of a genuine Sundelius job.

ED MOVED around in front of the bathroom doorway, with his gun ready. He kept his eyes glued to that shower sheet, and saw that it was swaying almost imperceptibly. The stand-up shower was in the side wall at the right, and he had only a side view of it. But he was squarely in the doorway of the bathroom, and the killer could see him if he peered through the crack in the middle.

Ed's gun covered the shower. He'd see the killer's gun, and he could fire his hair-trigger revolver a split-instant before the other. It was all the break he required. He stepped slowly into the bathroom. The sheet kept swaying. Then suddenly he heard the same sound he had heard before—only this time he was closer and he could identify it.

Distinct, unmistakable—it was a choked sob!

Swiftly, Ed stepped forward and yanked the sheet aside, thrusting the gun in front of him. Then he uttered an ejaculation of dismay.

This was no cold-eyed killer. It was only a huddled, sobbing, auburn-haired girl, who crouched against the wall and stared up at him with wide, frightened eyes. What further amazed Ed was that this girl was dressed only in flimsy panties and brassiere. A small bundle of clothes lay on the floor of the shower beside her—dress, shoes, hat and cloth coat.

The girl was sobbing aloud now. She started to get up slowly and tremulously, wrapping her arms about her breasts, flushing as she looked down at her own nakedness.

Ed Race smiled puzzledly. "You poor kid! What's happened to you?"

She raised her eyes to his, stopped sobbing, and her lips trembled. Suddenly she broke out in a gust of words that tumbled out with the frantic speed of approaching hysteria.

"Please, mister, I had to do it!" she cried. "They would have done terrible things to Frankie, if I didn't. Don't—don't think I'm bad. I only did it because I had to. The—the man said you wanted a divorce anyway, and it wasn't any disgrace to be a corre-spondent. He promised that he'd let Frankie alone, if I went through with it!"

She stepped out of the shower, and pulled the sheet around her timidly, gulping for breath.

Ed stared at her, amused. "But what's this terrible thing you've done, girlie?"

"I—I haven't done it yet. But—but I'm supposed to wait till you got here, then I'm supposed to come out l-like this, without any clothes on. That's when the detectives will come in, and then y-your wife can get her d-divorce—"

She couldn't finish. She dropped the shower sheet, raised both hands to her eyes, and began to sob.

Ed's mind was working swiftly, fitting odd pieces together—MacSpain detained on the 'phone, Sundelius just leaving the Clareton, his sardonic glance as he walked away, with that vague threat about Ed staying healthy. But a thing like this—how could it help Sundelius? How could it prevent his testifying against Conwell? Ed Race was a bachelor. He had no wife, no one to worry if he was caught in a room with a girl. Devious, unfathomable—this was like most of the traps laid by Duke Sundelius.

Ed took her gently by the arm, picked up her clothes from

the shower, and led her into the other room. "Who is making you do all this? And why do you have to do it? Who is Frankie, and what sort of trouble is he in?"

She picked up her dress, fumbling with it. "Frankie's my brother. He—he works for Smart and Smart, the jewelers. He—he's been playing the horses, and he took a couple of stones from the jewelry store and pawned them. Then some man came and told me about it, and Frankie admitted it. The man said that Frankie owed more money that he had lost at some gambling club, and that Frankie had two days to pay up. Yesterday, the man came and told me he'd forget what Frankie owes—and besides that he'd give Frankie enough money to take the stones out of pawn—provided I would do this thing."

"I see," Ed said softly. "What is your name, girlie?"

"Linton—Nellie Linton."

"And your brother would be Frank Linton?" Ed frowned.

He didn't wait for her answer. The bellhop had told him that the next room was occupied by a Frank Linton. The thing was growing quite clear in Ed's mind—diabolically clear. His eyes became bleak, hard. He gripped the girl's arm. "Never mind putting on that dress," he said. "How were you supposed to signal when you were ready for the detectives to break in?"

"By screaming," she said shakily.

"All right," Ed told her. "Now, do just as I say. Go ahead and scream—*quick!*"

She stared at him, open-mouthed.

"Scream, I tell you!" To hurry her up, Ed took her arm and pinched hard.

She cried out, and the scream had hardly died away when there was quick move meant at the corridor door and a key grated in the lock....

THE DOOR was pushed open and a voice out in the hall said, "Take a look, kid—and shoot fast, because he's lightning with a gun!" The door slammed violently inward, revealing a youth standing framed in the doorway. He was wild-eyed, and Ed could see that he had had several drinks too many.

Staring past the youth's shoulder, Ed caught a glimpse of a sardonic face that he recognized—Sam Myles, one of Duke Sundelius' mob. It was Myles whose voice Ed had heard urging the youth to shoot quick.

The young fellow had a gun in his hand, and stood there in the doorway, shivering with rage and hate, his hot eyes darting from the girl to Ed.

The girl uttered a cry. "Frankie! How—"

Frankie growled, never taking his eyes from Ed, "So you bring an eighteen-year-old kid up to your room!" His eyes swept back to Nellie Linton's nakedness. "My sister!" he exclaimed huskily. "This is too good for you, you rat—but take it!" His gun thrust forward.

Ed's revolver was already in his hand. He could have shot Frank Linton dead while the youth was still talking. Instead, he held his gun ready.

Linton had not taken Myles' advice literally, which showed that he was not a confirmed gunman. He should have shot without talking. Even then it was doubtful whether he could have beaten Ed to the trigger. But now he didn't have a chance.

Ed saw the lad's gun come forward, and his own finger steeled, ready to contract on the hair-trigger. But just then Nellie Linton uttered a shriek, and threw herself in front of Ed. "No, Frankie! It isn't what you think—"

Frank Linton cursed, and reached out to thrust his sister aside—and that was all Ed needed. He lunged forward with his .45. The muzzle caught Frank Linton on the side of the chin with a hard, thudding noise. The boy gasped, eyes rolling, knees wobbling. The gun fell from his fingers, and he collapsed.

That had been a ticklish lunge for Ed Race. His finger was still on the hair-trigger. He had had to slip it out and in again, *behind* the trigger to prevent the gun from going off and smashing Linton's face to smithereens. He didn't wait to watch Linton fall to the floor, but spring past him, reached the door in a stride and raced down the hall.

At the far end, Ed glimpsed Sammy Myles pulling open the fire-door. Myles was getting away by the stairs. He had kept young Linton in the next room, fed him liquor, then sent the boy in there to commit murder. It was clever. Ed Race would have been dead, and no one could have accused Sundelius of the murder. Myles would no doubt leave town, and the girl's story of having been induced to go through the act as a correspondent would be laughed out of court. Frank Linton would take the rap for the murder, and Conwell would go free because the main witness against him was dead....

All this flashed through Ed's mind as he saw Myles rushing through the fire exit. He snapped, "Hold it, Myles!"

The gunman realized his plan had gone wrong. He was around

the edge of the fire-door, and could have made his escape. But Ed's voice, calling after him, told him that the witness against Conwell was still alive. Viciously, he poked his head and shoulder back around the edge of the door. He thrust out the black snout of an automatic squarely at Ed, who was running toward him.

Ed's eyes were narrowed to pinpoints, as they always were when he fired at minute objects in his vaudeville number. A candle at the other end of a stage is a small target. But the edge of a man's shoulder, sticking out past a steel door, is bigger than a candle. He couldn't miss.

He fired as he ran, and the reverberation of the heavy .45 thundered in the narrow hallway, drowning out the scream of Sammy Myles.

Myles disappeared behind the door, his scream breaking off in the middle. When Ed got around that fire-door, Myles lay there, with blood streaming from his smashed shoulder. He was on his back, and his whipped, suddenly frightened eyes looked up at Ed without any of his usual swagger. Myles was no longer the deadly gunman, but only a yellow, cringing cur.

Ed's lips tightened, as he holstered his gun. He turned at the sound of the clanging elevator door, to meet Inspector MacSpain who was coming out of the cage, red-faced, gun in hand.

MACSPAIN BREATHED a sigh of relief when he saw Ed on his own two feet. "God!" he exclaimed. "I thought that was you getting yours, Ed! That 'phone call was a put-up job. Some mug kept stringing me along offering to stool for me, and, when I got wise, I tried to have the call traced, and wasted time. I should have known it was a plant. What happened?"

Swiftly, Ed told him everything. "Those two kids are in the room now, Mac," he finished. "Give the boy a break. Don't take him in. I have an idea."

MacSpain bent over the moaning Myles, and picked up his automatic. "Yellow, like the rest of them!" he grunted. "That was good shooting, Ed. What's your idea?"

The elevator boy was googling at them, and several doors on the corridor had opened.

Ed said quickly, "Help me get Myles into the room. Come on, lift him up. What do we care if he bleeds to death?"

Myles yelled, as they lifted him, "Gawd, it's killing me! Get a doctor! A doctor!"

They carried him, none too gently, into the room, and placed him on the bed.

Nellie Linton was on the floor, holding her brother's head in her lap, and applying a wet handkerchief to his chin. She looked up as they brought Myles in, and said, "That's the man who made me come here."

Ed nodded with satisfaction. "Go in the next room, Mac," he said to the inspector, "and call the switchboard. Tell the operator to fix it so you can listen in on the call I'm going to make."

MacSpain glanced at him, puzzled, then shrugged. "It's your show, Ed. I'll tell Regan, the house dick, to stand at the door and not let anybody in—if you want privacy."

"You guessed it, Mac," Ed told him ominously. "I want privacy!"

Myles stirred in the bed, holding his shoulder, his hand crimson. "Gawd, what you gonna do? Why don't you get a doctor?"

MacSpain grinned sourly and went out without answering him.

Ed came over to the bed, holding his .45. He looked down dispassionately at the wounded gunman. "Sammy, do you remember a night two years ago when the police found the body of a man in an empty lot in Brooklyn? It was a man who had welched on a bet with Duke Sundelius. He'd been shot in the shoulder, and then some one had played with him for a long while. The medical examiner said that some one had kept striking his wounded shoulder many times, with a blunt instrument—till the man died. Do you remember that case, Sammy? They could never pin it on you, but it doesn't matter. It gives me an idea."

Sammy Myles' face was drained of blood, in sharp contrast to the crimson sheet upon which he lay. "Gawd! What you gonna do?"

Ed hefted the revolver, experimentally. "I'm going to try that treatment on you, Sammy. I'm going to pound that smashed shoulder of yours, with the butt of my revolver. I'm going to keep on pounding till you faint. Then I'm going to revive you, and do it all over again. I'm going to keep it up till you die. Then I'll tell the police that you tried to escape and I hit you in the scuffle. The medical examiner won't be particular about a rat like you."

Myles gasped, "No—you wouldn't do that, Race! Gawd, no!"

Ed nodded coolly. "That's what I'm going to do. And here's the first little love tap." He raised the gun.

Myles screeched. *"Please—no!* Don't hit me. I—know what you want. I'll—talk."

Ed smiled. "I want more than talk, Sammy. I want you to call your boss, Sundelius, and report to him. I want you to make believe that your little plan went off okay, and I want you to report like that. Well?"

Myles was sweating copiously. His eyes were fixed in terrified fascination upon the revolver which Ed swung significantly. "What about me? Do I get off easy—"

"You get off with a nice jail term," Ed told him coldly, "and a doctor to treat your wound so you won't die. But I want you to do this so that Sundelius gets the chair."

Myles opened his mouth, closed it, opened it again, and said in a whisper, "Gimme the 'phone...."

ED SMILED, hiding his relief. He would never have been able to give Myles the harsh treatment he had promised. He handed the wounded man the 'phone, waited while he got Duke at the Sundelius Club. Then Ed bent close so he could hear the conversation at both ends.

Myles said, "Hello, Duke. This is me—Sammy."

"Yes?" Duke's voice was tight. "Did it go off all right?"

"Okay, boss. I fixed it so the Linton kid would barge in on Race at the right minute. I filled the kid full of liquor, and he plugged Race." Myles looked up at Ed, then added into the 'phone, embellishing the story, "Race plugged the kid, too. That fixes everything, and Conwell can't fry for knocking off Opperman. Sonny sure did a lousy job on Opperman, boss. He should have waited till he was sure no one saw him. But now we had to get Race knocked off—"

"Shut up, you fools!" Duke's voice raged. "Don't you realize you're talking over the 'phone? The wire might be tapped. I ought to have you knocked off, too—"

Duke's tirade broke off with a gasp, as Inspector MacSpain's voice, from the 'phone in the next room, cut in, "That's swell, Duke. This conversation is just what I wanted. We can pin murder on you now, without waiting to convict Sonny Conwell. I'll be right over for you!"

Duke Sundelius screamed hoarsely into the 'phone, "You damned double-crossing rat, Myles! I'll skin you alive if I have to chase you around the world!" Then suddenly he hung up.

Ed took the instrument from Myles' hand, and put it back on the night table Myles sighed wearily, and fainted. Ed turned just in time to see MacSpain, grinning, rush into the room.

The inspector was jubilant. "That cleans up Sundelius! It'll get him cold—"

"Why did you warn him on the 'phone?" Ed demanded. "You're giving him a chance to escape!"

MacSpain winked at him. "Do you think old Mac is that dumb, Ed?" He reached for the 'phone, which had just begun to ring. "That'll be for me." He picked it up, said crisply, "MacSpain speaking." He listened for a moment. "All right, Flannery," he said at length. "Call the M.E. and the morgue wagon. I'll be over in a little while."

He hung up, turned to Ed, who was listening, mystified. MacSpain rubbed his hands in satisfaction. "I took the precaution," he explained to Ed, "to post a dozen men around the Sundelius Club before I got myself hooked up with your 'phone. After that scare I gave Sundelius, did you hear how fast he hung up? He must have realized we would be coming for him. So he packed up all his ready cash and tried to lam out the back way, with Sonny Conwell. My men called to them to halt, but unfortunately—"MacSpain's tone became unctuous—"Sundelius and Conwell refused to surrender and attempted to run. The boys had to kill them!"

Ed Race's eyes were gleaming. "My congratulations, Inspector. It looks like your life work has been consummated!" He was attracted by the sound of sobbing from the floor in the middle of the room. It was the Linton boy and girl.

"What'll we do with these two kids?" he asked MacSpain.

Nellie came over and put a trembling hand on Ed's arm. "Y-you're not going to be hard on Frankie, are you?"

Ed shook his head. "How much was that stuff worth that you took and pawned, Frank?" he asked.

The lad raised his head, revealing bloodshot eyes. He was holding his jaw where Ed had hit him. "I—I pawned them for fifty dollars."

Ed nodded. "I see." He came over and stood above Frank Linton. "Now look, Frankie, you can talk freely, because Inspector MacSpain isn't listening." He turned and glared at the inspector.

MACSPAIN WAS a policeman—but even more than that. He understood the difference between vicious criminals like Sundelius, and young babes like the Lintons who are forced into crime by the wolves who prey on innocence. He knew also, that the law, unfortunately, does not make a careful distinction. Before a court, Linton could get two years, if found guilty of stealing fifty dollars worth of stones. Those two years might make the lad a confirmed criminal.

He hesitated, glanced from Ed to the girl, then to Frankie. At last, he sighed.

Ed grinned, and turned back to Linton. "There's no charge against you here," he said. "I'm not signing any complaint against you. Now here's sixty dollars. That ought to cover the interest, too. Go and get those stones out of hock, and put them back in the store. If I catch you gambling or stealing again, I'll whale the hide off you!"

Frank Linton stared up at him, unbelievingly. "You're giving me that money?" He took it fearfully, as if he were afraid that it would crumble in his fingers. "I swear to you, Mr. Race, that I'll never gamble again in my life."

Nellie Linton was crying softly. She came over and took Ed's hand, and kissed it. Ed laughed, and put his arm around her, and gave her a hug. "And don't you go being a correspondent any more, either!"

MURDER MATINEE

IT WAS eight minutes to three when Ed Race got to the Citizens' Deposit National Bank. He glanced up and down Broadway, looking for old Sam Mingo, but at first didn't see him. Then he saw a cab at the curb, and another one pulled up about fifty feet behind it. From the first of the two taxis Sam Mingo now got out.

Mingo, the clown.... Ed had seen the old man do his clown act on the vaudeville circuits for ten years now, and God knew how long he had been doing it before that—before Ed had joined the Partages Circuit, himself, as the Masked Marksman. Mingo was a little slow lately—his joints weren't so flexible. But he still managed to give the crowds a good fifteen minutes of side-splitting fun.

Now, however, there was no levity in Sam Mingo's countenance. His wrinkled face was pale, and a quick, urgent fear showed in his eyes.

"I knew I could count on you, Ed!" was his greeting.

Ed Race's lips tightened. "I don't know what you want the money for, Sam, and I'm not asking. You can have it, of course. But I can see you're in some kind of trouble. Maybe, if you told me the whole thing, I could help."

They were inside the bank now, Ed writing a check at one of the accommodation desks along the wall.

Mingo the clown smiled sadly. "No, Ed. This is something I've got to face myself. There's no one I'd rather tell than you—but I've got to keep it to myself."

Ed nodded. "Just remember, if you *should* need help." He walked over to the teller's window, slid the check in.

The teller raised his eyebrows. "How'll you have it, Mr. Race?"

Ed threw a questioning look at Mingo, and the old clown said, "In hundreds."

In a moment they were walking away from the cage, and Ed handed Mingo five thousand dollars in hundred-dollar bills. "There it is, Sam—and I hope it helps you."

Mingo sighed. "To tell you the truth, Ed, I don't know if it will. I—I may not live to see the end." He thrust a slip of paper at Ed. "Here's my note for five thousand. I have insurance. If anything should happen to me, you can collect from my estate."

Ed took the slip of paper, folded and put it in his pocket without a glance. "If anything should happen to you, Sam," he said softly, "I'll see that whoever is responsible pays double."

They were in the street again, and suddenly, Ed felt the old man's slight figure stiffen beside him. His glance followed Mingo's wide-eyed stare, and he, himself, became taut. He swung forward slightly, on the balls of his feet. His shoulders hunched forward, almost imperceptibly, so that the weight of the two shoulder holsters, sheathing the twin .45's under his armpits, moved forward, with the butts of the guns almost peeping out from under his coat lapels. His eyes, narrowed almost to slits, were fixed upon the two men who had just emerged from the taxicab parked behind Mingo's.

Ed could see old Mingo taking

a terrible beating!

Ed's lips hardly moved, but the name he uttered was distinctly heard by the old man beside him. "Moulson!"

The taller man, whose name Ed had breathed, had a patch over his right eye. He was long, gaunt, narrow-waisted and narrow-shouldered. His companion was stocky, his thick neck bulged out of a tight collar—and his eyes were those of a killer.

Mingo said hurriedly, "The short one with Moulson is Milo Tyker. He's as bad as Moulson." Suddenly Mingo's voice broke. "God! I didn't realize they had followed me!"

Ed Race didn't take his eyes from the two men approaching. "Can I do something for you?" he asked old Mingo.

"Yes, yes, Ed. It—it's deadly important that I get away from here in my cab, without being followed by Moulson and Tyker. It—it means everything to me. I hate to ask you, Ed, but do you think you could… detain them?"

Ed's eyes were glowing. "I can detain them," he said.

MOULSON AND Tyker were abreast of them now, having pushed through the moving pedestrians on Broadway. Moulson's cadaverous eyes had flicked carelessly over Ed Race; and he nudged Tyker, who moved up in such a way that he stood almost alongside Ed. The thick-necked man's hand slid into his jacket pocket.

Moulson paid no more attention to Ed, as if he were sure that Tyker would easily dispose of him. His cadaverous eyes rested ironically on the bulge in Mingo's coat over the breast pocket, where the package of money lay. "Looks like you've drawn some money, Mingo. Where were you going with it?"

Mingo said, "Damn you, Moulson, leave me alone. You've done me enough harm as it is."

Moulson's lips were sneering. "I'm not leaving you alone, clown, till you've talked to me—told me what I want to know." His gnarled hand came out and gripped Mingo's arm, so that the old man winced. "If you want to call the police, it's all right with me. But you're not calling any police. We're sticking with you till we get what we want."

Ed Race took one short step backward, which brought Tyker in front of him. "You're mistaken, Moulson," Ed said mildly. "You're not sticking with him. He's getting in that cab, and driving away. You're going to stay here—not follow him."

Moulson's eyes had switched to him the moment Ed began to talk. "You better stay out of this," he said, "if you want to remain healthy. You know who I am, fellow?"

Ed watched both Moulson and Tyker. Tyker's hand was slowly coming out of his jacket pocket. "Yes, I know who you are, Moulson," Ed said. "You're a murderer—but the police have never been able to get anything on you. This little gunman of yours does most of your dirty work, together with a half dozen more. You've got good lawyers, and plenty of money. But all that won't help you if you're dead. I promise you that you'll be dead sixty seconds after you start anything."

Ed had spoken in a cool, deliberate voice, as if he were discussing the condition of the stock market. But his eyes had gone a blank slate-gray, become cold and bleak. He said to Tyker, "I wouldn't pull that gun all the way out, if I were you. Maybe if I tell you who *I* am, it'll explain why. For your information, I'm Ed Race."

Tyker's face went white. He gulped. His hand checked in his pocket. Moulson's face showed no emotion whatsoever, but there was just a little stiffening of his gaunt jaw.

Both knew Ed Race by reputation, as did all of the underworld. Ed Race, the Masked Marksman of vaudeville fame, who received top billing in all the vaudeville circuits of the country, who performed incredible feats of marksmanship on the stage, who juggled with six heavy .45 caliber, hair-trigger revolvers—the way another might juggle dumbbells.

They knew, too, that Ed Race could use those guns offstage as well as onstage. They knew that his insatiable appetite for adventure had sent him into the field of criminology, as a side line. They had heard of deadly killers who had gone up against Ed Race, and never lived to tell just how fast those two .45's of his had leaped out at them, bucking, roaring, belching flame and death. Ed Race held licenses to operate as a private detective in a dozen states. He never used them to make money, because he earned far more than he needed on the stage. But he was, nevertheless, more deadly than a mercenary detective, for it was his friends only whom he helped, and he hated the wolves who preyed on them....

THAT WAS why Tyker's hand slid back into his pocket, and why small beads of sweat began to stand out on the stocky gunman's forehead. But his small eyes mirrored the vicious hate that was festering in his rat-like killer's soul. He was a killer—

but he wasn't going to try his luck against the Masked Marksman until he got more than an even break.

Moulson said jerkily, "Damn you, Tyker, I thought you had guts. Keep him from interfering. They won't dare to call the police—will you, Mingo?"

Old Sam Mingo's face was haggard. "You'd better forget it, Ed. I—I don't want trouble."

Ed Race laughed harshly. He took another step backward, with his hands at his side. "You're going away from here, Sam, alone—whether you like it or not. Go on—get in that cab, and drive away. If these men try to follow you, I'll stop them. If they fight, I'll shoot them."

Moulson sneered. "We're not threatening you, Race. If you shoot, you'll go to the chair. It'll be murder."

Ed smiled thinly. "We'll see about that." He gave Sam Mingo a little push. "Go on!"

Dazed, almost unwillingly, the old man started toward the cab at the curb. It seemed that there was someone in there who had been waiting all this time, for the door was opened from inside.

Moulson threw a quick, worried glance at Ed, and started to go after Mingo.

Ed Race took a quick step forward, seized Moulson by the collar, swung him around violently and sent him spinning back against the wall of the bank building.

Moulson screeched, "Tyker! Get him! He attacked first!"

Ed Race stood there, smiling coldly, his eyes bleak and gray, his hands loose at his sides.

He was ready.

Tyker had seized the opportunity while Ed's eyes were off him, to get the gun out of his pocket. It was halfway up now, and he was snarling, eyes red with killing lust, his confidence supreme that Ed couldn't beat him to the draw. No living man could have drawn a gun and fired it in the flashing split-second of time that it would take for Tyker's automatic to come up that fraction of an inch and belch lead into Ed's body.

But Ed Race had more than one trick up his sleeve. On the stage, from coast to coast he was used to performing miracles of acrobatic marksmanship. His favorite number—one that never failed to bring down the house—was to juggle his six revolvers in the air, get them all up high at once, then do a back-somersault. As he came out of that back-flip, he would catch the descending revolvers one at a time, fire each one once—and each shot invariably extinguished the flame of one of a row of candles at the other end of the stage. In ten years, he had never missed a candle. A wealthy skeptic had once followed him from town to town for a year, watching each performance and waiting for him to miss. The skeptic had finally gone home—convinced.

Now, on Broadway and Forty-Eighth Street, with pedestrians passing, Ed Race gave the same performance—but with far more at stake than the gratification of an audience.

Under Tyker's eyes, Ed suddenly fell into a disconcerting back-somersault that carried him ten feet away along the sidewalk. Tyker's gun exploded, and the slug shrieked in the air where Ed had been, flashed past pedestrians, and flattened itself against the masonry of the building opposite.

Tyker's eyes bulged, trying to follow Ed's swiftly moving

figure. He lowered the muzzle of the gun for another shot, but he never pulled the trigger. Ed Race was coming to his feet now, and there was a gun in his hand. Still in motion, he snapped a single shot. The heavy .45 thundered in the street, and a woman screamed. The scream mingled with the deep-toned detonation of the revolver, and drowned out the agonized screech that burst from Tyker's throat. Blood gushed from the spot under his chin where Ed's slug had caught him. The automatic fell, and his empty hands clawed at his throat for the fraction of an instant as he went hurtling backward from the force of the impact. Then he fell flat on his back on the pavement, twitched, and lay still.

Ed swung his gun toward Moulson, but the gaunt man still lay where he had fallen, hands raised in the air.

Ed Race uttered a short, brittle laugh, and turned away from Moulson, contemptuously slipping his gun into its holster.

THE CROWD which had gathered stared at Ed with wide, amazed eyes. They had just seen him kill a man, and yet there was no faintest sign of emotion in his face. He was not immediately recognized, for though many of these people had seen him on the stage, he always appeared masked. But they had witnessed those swift instants of deadly action, had seen him shoot down a man about to fire at him. They connected that exhibition of lightning-like motion with the legends that were already rife about Ed Race. Here and there in the crowd ran whispers, "It's the Masked Marksman. He's at the Clyde Theater this week…. They say he's death on crooks…. Looks like those stories are true they tell about him!"

Ten minutes later, there were squad cars, headquarters

men, reporters and photographers. A shooting on Broadway was a matter for headlines. And naturally, dour old Inspector MacSpain arrived.

MacSpain had worked with Ed Race several times in the past. He grimaced when he recognized the dead man.

"Tyker, eh?" There were crinkles around his eyes. "The city ought to pay you to stay in town, Ed. If you stuck around Broadway for a year, there wouldn't be any mobsters left."

There were a dozen witnesses eager to testify that the killing was self-defense. No one was really sorry that Tyker was dead. Ed said nothing about Mingo.... Neither did Moulson. Queerly, Moulson in his statement said that Tyker had attacked Ed in the street *without provocation....*

Ed raised his eyebrows when he heard Moulson dictate that to the police stenographer. He looked up to find MacSpain watching him quizzically—and Moulson threw him a vitriolic glance as he left.

IT WAS late in the afternoon when Ed left headquarters, after the district attorney's office sent over word that there would be no prosecution.

MacSpain walked out to the street with him. "Look here, Ed," the inspector said. "There's something that you and Moulson haven't told. There's something you're both hiding." MacSpain jabbed a forefinger into Ed's chest. "I'm the one that got the D.A. to drop this thing. He could just as easily have made you stand trial. Of course," he added hastily, "I grant you would never have been convicted. But it would have been damned inconvenient for you."

Ed grinned at him. "Think how silly the D.A.'s office and the police department would have looked, prosecuting a man for killing a gunman like Tyker!"

MacSpain nodded. "That's right, Ed. But remember, I saved you a lot of trouble. You know I always play ball with you. Don't you want to talk to me about—anything else?"

Ed shook his head. "Sorry, Mac."

The inspector glanced at him shrewdly. "I talked to some of the people around the bank building. I talked to the teller in the bank. He says you were in there a minute or two before the shooting, with another man. Somebody in the street identified that man as Sam Mingo. Sam Mingo lives in the same hotel you live in. Yet you met him at the bank."

MacSpain lowered his voice. "All right, you don't have to talk, Ed. But I just want to tell you this: There was a bank job pulled last month. You may have read about it in the papers. Two hundred grand in negotiable securities was grabbed. We don't know who did the job. But we're damned certain—morally— that Moulson was behind it, and is going to fence the stuff when it cools off. Now—" MacSpain's voice took on an edge it had not had before—"if this shooting this afternoon had anything to do with that bank job, Ed, it wouldn't be smart of you to hold out on me."

Ed said, "I give you my word I know nothing about that job, Mac. I read about it—the Intercontinental Trust. But I'm sure this doesn't connect. I'll tell you this much. Sam Mingo is in some sort of trouble, and he doesn't want the police—"

MacSpain nodded dourly. "I could have told you. His son

has disappeared. He's up in Missing Persons—reported by his fiancée, Nola Anglin."

Ed's eyes grew thoughtful. He could trust MacSpain. "I wonder if that's why Mingo borrowed five thousand from me this afternoon."

MacSpain smiled. "Thanks for telling me. I knew it from the bank teller."

On the way back to the hotel, Ed wondered if he should have told MacSpain that Mingo had been mortally afraid of Moulson and Tyker, that the two of them had seemed to possess some sort of hold on the old man. He shrugged, and dismissed the matter. He was satisfied that Mingo had gotten away without being followed. There had been someone in the cab with the old man—Ed had caught a glimpse of a woman's hand on the door.

But that was all. If Mingo needed the money for a woman, then that was all right with Ed, too.

Ed reached the Hillmont.

HE WAS just washing the razor when the 'phone in the bedroom rang. Ed turned off the water, came out of the bathroom, and the bell tinkled twice more before he got to it. He picked it up and spoke into the transmitter. But there was only a faint gurgle at the other end, followed by a flat, slapping sound.

Ed frowned, and said 'hello' once more, in a slightly irritated voice. He waited a moment, was about to jiggle the hook, when a smooth voice spoke into the receiver: "Is this Room Fourteen-ten?"

Ed said, "No. This is Eight-four-six."

"Sorry. I got the wrong room. Will you hang up please?"

Ed Race's eyes narrowed. That voice sounded troublesomely familiar. He had heard it somewhere recently, but couldn't place it. He laid the 'phone back in the cradle, waited a moment, then picked it up again. Something was happening here.

The operator down at the switchboard answered, and Ed said, "Someone rang here just now. Did the call come from outside?"

"No, sir. I handled that call myself. It was from Room Eleven-o-five, upstairs."

Ed tensed. "That's Mr. Mingo's room, isn't it?" He didn't wait for her to answer. "But it wasn't Mr. Mingo talking. Did that party ask for me, or for Room Fourteen-ten?"

"He asked for you, Mr. Race, and I'm sure it was Mr. Mingo himself. I know his voice."

Ed thanked her, and hung up. He moved fast now. He didn't bother with shirt or tie. He slung on his shoulder holsters, put on his coat, and made tracks for the corridor, where he punched the *Up* button. His face was grim, bleak, as the cage deposited him on the eleventh floor.

There was a *Do Not Disturb* sign on the knob of 1105. But the radio was going full blast inside. Ed opened his coat over his undershirt, so that the shoulder holsters swung loose. He rapped on the door.

The radio stopped playing abruptly. Someone inside growled, "Yes?"

Ed's lips tightened. It wasn't Mingo's voice. He said, "It's the bellboy, Mr. Mingo. I have your suit from the tailor's."

There was a moment of silence, then the voice inside said testily, "Can't you see the sign? Bring it back later."

Almost at once, the radio began to bleat.

Ed Race glanced down the hall, desperately. He had recognized the voice now. It was Moulson... Moulson, in there with Mingo, and the radio going....

THIS WAS the west wing of the hotel. It fronted on Broadway, and there was a setback here on the eleventh floor. Ed knew, because he had occupied rooms on almost every one of the Hillmont's floors in his many stops in New York. Now he walked swiftly down the corridor to the end window. It was frosted glass, shut tight. Ed tried to raise it, but it wouldn't budge.

Ed took off his hat, wrapped it around the butt of his revolver, and smashed at the glass. It fell outward, tinkling on the pebbled ledge. He chipped away the rough edges, stepped through and climbed out on the ledge. It was a six-foot wide setback, high up over Broadway, and from here one could see uninterruptedly across the Hudson and over the Palisades. But Ed wasted no time on the view. Pebbles crunched under his feet as he moved along the wall toward Sam Mingo's window. The shade was drawn but there was a light behind it, and the raucous sound of the radio was even plainer here.

Ed wasn't looking anywhere but at the window, so that he failed to notice the dark shape which had suddenly moved away into the shadows. Now however, he detected a faint hint of motion, and his hand streaked in and out from his shoulder holster.

Then he uttered a low ejaculation of bewilderment. The shape had resolved itself into the slim figure of a young woman.

Even in the comparative darkness of the ledge out here, Ed recognized her at once. "Nola Anglin!" he exclaimed.

She had begun to back away, but at the sound of his voice she stopped. She was clutching a long envelope to her breast.

Her picture had been in all the papers a week or so ago—Nola Anglin, the new star in the operatic firmament. At twenty-five, she was to sing Aida at the Metropolitan. She had just started her career, but the critics already prophesied a glorious future for her… and here was Nola Anglin, on the terrace outside the window of a vaudeville clown!

Ed looked into her eyes, and saw there fright and a panic that bordered on hysteria. She started to say, "They—they're killing him in there—"

But Ed Race had already turned away from her. He knelt at the window, and peered in through the half-inch between the bottom of the shade and the sill. His body grew taut, and his hand tightened on his gun.

Sam Mingo was taking a terrible beating to the accompaniment of the radio. The old man was on the floor between the bed and the window. He was on his face, arms thrown up over his head.

One of the two men was Moulson. The other was a small man with a bald head. They were both working over Sam Mingo. The bald-headed man had a gun in his hand, and was bringing the barrel of it down rhythmically, methodically, in slashes to the bare back of Sam Mingo.

Mingo's shirt had been torn from his back and Ed Race could see the long gashes where the barrel of the bald man's gun had raked him. Little ridges of muscle stood out at the sides of Ed Race's jaw as he watched the beating. He stepped back from the window, and reversed his gun, raising it to smash the glass.

Before he could strike, he felt a tug at his arm. Nola Anglin was close to him.

"No, no!" Her voice, though still pitched low, assumed a note of frantic desperation. "You—you mustn't."

Ed growled deep in his throat. He shoved her with his elbow. "Get out of the way!"

SHE GASPED with the pain of the blow, but she was right back, before Ed could lift the gun again. Her arms went about his hand, dragged it down, held it tight against her breasts. "You mustn't. I tell you—you mustn't go in there." Her voice grew desperate, pleading. "I know who you are. I saw you today when you went to the bank with Sam to get cash for him. I was waiting in the cab." Her words tumbled over one another.

"You're Ed Race, the Masked Marksman," she said. "You're a killer, too. I know about the men you've killed—criminals. Those two are the same—they deserve to be killed. But this time you must stay out of it. If you kill them—you'll break old Sam's heart!"

Ed stared down at her white face. "I almost believe you," he muttered. "But why? Why are they beating him? Why must I let it go on?"

"I—I can't tell you," she stammered.

Ed looked at her closely, searchingly. "You're engaged to young Charlie Mingo. What has all this to do with him?"

He raised his clubbed gun once more, and she uttered a desperate cry. "Wait!"

The words came tumbling out, once more. But her eyes were lowered, her fingers fumbling at the envelope. "Sam wouldn't want me to tell you. But he also wouldn't want you to interfere. It's about Charlie. Charlie was drunk and took part in a bank robbery. Moulson and Tyker, and this man here—Kelder—were all in it. After they'd made their getaway, Charlie realized what a terrible thing he'd done, and wouldn't go through with it. He got away from Tyker and Kelder, and took the loot with him. He was going to return it."

She looked up at him, and shuddered. "I—I can hardly go on—"

Ed said gently, "You don't have to. I understand the rest. Charlie wants to return the bonds, and leave the country. Old Sam borrowed the five thousand from me, to send him away with. And Moulson is trying to make Sam tell him where Charlie's hiding out!"

She nodded. "Can't you see why Sam doesn't want interference? If the police came in on it, and if Kelder and Moulson are arrested, they'll talk first, knowing that Charlie is going to turn back the bonds anyway."

Ed's lips were tight. "So he's taking a beating for that son of his! And you—"

Her face was pale in the semi-darkness. "It's not for Charlie any more. It's because of old Sam. I've come to know him well since I've been engaged to Charlie. I love him like a father. I've learned to respect his fierce pride in his name. It's to save his name that I was going to help get Charlie out of the country. He gave me the money you loaned him, and we were making our final plans, when Moulson and Kelder arrived. I had just 'phoned Charlie at his hideaway, told him I was coming right over."

She went on. "Then when those two arrived suddenly, Sam pushed me out here on the ledge, and opened the door for them. He thought he could hold them here while I made my way out of the hotel to Charlie. But when he saw they meant to torture him, he tried to call you, and they stopped him. I—I saw everything from the window here, and I couldn't go...."

Ed cursed under his breath. Some one was pounding at the corridor of Sam Mingo's room.

Ed threw a quick glance at Nola Anglin, then dropped to his knees to peer under the shade....

HE SAW the man, Kelder, turning off the radio. Moulson had a gun out now, too. He motioned to Kelder to open the corridor door, while he, himself, stepped behind it.

Old Sam Mingo raised his bloody back from the floor, and shouted something toward that door. Ed heard part of what he said, "Get away! They'll kill you...."

Then the door was open, and a young man came barging into the room.

Ed heard Nola Anglin's, "Charlie!"

Inside the room, Kelder gave ground before the furious entrance of Charlie Mingo. Charlie was carrying a thick brief-case under one arm, and had an automatic in his other hand. He didn't bother to look behind him, didn't see Moulson was stealing up at his back.

Ed Race jumped to his feet. His gun butt smashed at the windowpane, crashing the glass inward. Then he reached in and yanked the shade off the roller. The room was revealed to him, its occupants frozen in the positions he had last seen them—even to Moulson with the raised gun butt in his hand.

Ed had both his revolvers out now, and squeezed the trigger of the right hand weapon. It thundered, bucking and kicking in his hand. A round black hole appeared in Kelder's forehead. He twisted around ludicrously, slumped down.

Charlie Mingo stood petrified, but Moulson jumped back, sheltered by Charlie's body, and reversed his gun again, so that he was holding it by the butt. He kept behind Charlie Mingo, and shouted.

"Stay out there, Race, or I'll kill Mingo's kid!"

Old Sam, still on the floor, raised a grief-stricken face to his son. "Charlie! Why did you have to come—"

Charlie Mingo said, "Hell, Dad, I'm rotten—but not rotten enough to let you take this rap for me. I figured they'd work on you—"

He whirled suddenly, and poked his gun at Moulson, pulling the trigger three times quickly. But Moulson had already backed out into the corridor, and ducked around the lintel. Charlie Mingo's shots missed him. Moulson's gun came around the edge of the door, and he fired once.

Charlie staggered backward.

And then Ed Race was in the room, leaping over the dead body of Kelder, over the struggling figure of old Sam Mingo, past Charlie, and out into the corridor.

Moulson was down the end, near the fire-exit. He couldn't get the fire-door opened. He turned, snarling like a trapped rat and raised his gun.

Ed Race laughed a deep, booming laugh, and fired once with his left hand gun. Moulson shrieked, and fell forward. Ed turned away without looking at him a second time. He had aimed for the man's heart, and he knew he had hit.

He disregarded the craning necks in a half-dozen suddenly opened doors.

Old Sam Mingo and Nola Anglin were bending over young Charlie, who lay on the floor on his back, with blood gurgling out of a wound high up on the left side of his chest.

There were tears coursing down Nola's cheeks, but old Sam Mingo's face was white and expressionless. His back was raw and bleeding, but he didn't seem to feel it. He had his son's head cradled in his arms. Charlie smiled faintly behind the blood.

He gasped hoarsely, "This is the best way Dad. At least, I'm going out like a—man!" Then his head fell back, dead.

SAM MINGO stayed there on the floor, cradling his son's head. Nola Anglin got up, listlessly. She was still holding the envelope. She extended it to Ed Race. "That's the money you lent Sam," she said in a dry voice. "It was to take Charlie out of the country."

Silently, Ed pocketed the envelope. He heard the crowd that was peering in through the open door, heard a brittle, authoritative voice, and turned to see Inspector MacSpain pushing through.

"It's that Intercontinental Trust case, Mac. Young Charlie

Mingo here, got on to the fact that Moulson and this bird were the ones who pulled that job. He trailed them, and somehow he got the bonds away from them. They came here to torture his whereabouts out of Sam. Charlie and I got here in time."

MacSpain said skeptically, "I see." He took the briefcase which Ed handed him, and peered inside. The bonds were there. MacSpain's face cleared.

Old Sam Mingo took Ed's hand, and pressed it. "Thanks for that lie, Ed. Thanks for keeping the name clean. I'm only a clown—but—" his eyes watered—"well, I'm glad my son didn't die with a rogue's name." He swayed a little.

"Keep your chin up," Ed said. "We both go on tonight at the Clyde!"

The eyes of Mingo the Clown were misted. But he straightened his shoulders, quieted the twitching muscles in his face. "That's right," he muttered. "We have a curtain." He laughed hollowly. "On with the Show!"

Ed Race and Nola Anglin led him gently into the next room, where a doctor was waiting to treat his raw back, so he would not be late for his curtain call.

DEATH BOOKS THE SHOW

THE TELEPHONE call for Tom Kirby came about five minutes after Ed Race had finished his number at the Clyde Theater. Ed was in his dressing room, changing to street clothes. He heard Boiling, the assistant stage manager, come past his door and knock at the door of Kirby's dressing room.

"Call for you, Tom," Boiling called out. "On the pay telephone behind the property room."

Ed Race heard Kirby's reply, heard the acrobat come out of his room and go to answer the call. At the moment, he attached no special significance to it. He finished dressing and packed away four of the six heavy revolvers he used in his own act. The other two he placed in the holsters under his arms. He never went out without those two .45 calibre revolvers—they had become as much a part of him as his necktie. The last act of the vaudeville show was on now, and Ed could hear the fast tempo of the orchestra as it kept time to the twin xylophones of the Peterman Brothers out on the stage. He was about to go out into the wings and take a look at the crack xylophonists, when there was a quick knock at the door, and it was pushed open almost at once.

Tom Kirby came in like a gale of wind. Ed looked at him keenly, saw that the acrobat was breathing hard. His face was

She kicked the gun toward Ed Race!

dead white, his lips trembling. His eyes were lit up with a queer mad light.

Kirby left the door open and gripped Ed Race by the arm. "Look here, Ed, I want to borrow one of your guns!"

He pushed past him to the small leather case on the dressing table, which was still open, revealing the four beautiful, hair-trigger revolvers.

"Hey! Wait a minute, Tom," Ed said. "You were all right a minute ago, and then you got that telephone call. Now you want a gun. You haven't a license—"

"I have! Here…." With trembling fingers, Tom Kirby pulled a wallet out of his pocket, exhibited his license to carry a gun. "But I haven't the time to go home and get my own. I—I'm in a hurry."

Ed watched him with narrow eyes. "What's the idea? Want to kill someone?"

Tom Kirby had one of the revolvers out of the box. He spun the barrel to see if it was loaded, then turned to face Ed. "You're damned right I do! I'm going to kill that rat, Carlos Esquibar! By God, I don't care if I burn for it!"

Kirby pushed toward the door, but Ed Race planted himself in front of the angry acrobat. "You're mad, Tom! You aren't going to commit murder!"

Kirby gave him a short, hard laugh. "Call it murder if you like. That oily Portugee got my daughter to run away with him, didn't he? He talked her into quitting the act, leaving me, and marrying him. I lost track of her for two years—then I heard of them in New Orleans. If I hadn't sent her money, he'd have made her go on the streets!"

ED RACE listened sympathetically. Tom Kirby hadn't been the same ever since the day his daughter, Ellen, eloped with Carlos the Magician. Tom had made a trouper of Ellen, had taught her all the tricks of a big-time vaudeville acrobatic team.

Her mother had been dead for many years, and Tom Kirby had been both a father and mother to Ellen. Then Carlos the Magician had come along, had fascinated the eighteen-year-old girl with his smile and his big talk, and she had eloped with him.

Everybody knew Carlos' record. Two convictions on vice charges; a short term in Atlanta on a lottery charge; before that, a round dozen of prohibition and drug arrests. But Ellen Kirby, blind to all that, had gone with Carlos Esquibar—yielding to the fascination that this man of forty knew only too well how to exert upon an impressionable girl of eighteen.

Ed's sympathy was all for Tom Kirby. He knew what his friend had gone through, thinking, in the long hours of the night, about his only daughter and the man who had wrecked her life.

Tom Kirby tried to get past him through the door. He was not trembling so much now, but there was a cold resolution in his eyes that Ed recognized well enough. "I swore I'd kill that Portugee, Ed, and I'm going to do it. I've had a private detective agency on the lookout for him for a year. And just now I got a call from one of their operatives. He's spotted Esquibar, with another man, standing outside Gallipoli's Restaurant, on Broadway!"

Ed Race blocked the doorway. "If you think I'm letting you go out with that gun, Tom, to deliberately commit murder, you're crazy. Let me handle it," he pleaded. "I'll go and talk to Esquibar, make him tell me where Ellen is. Maybe I can talk him into giving her a divorce—"

Tom Kirby grunted, waving the gun. "Like hell you will, Ed.

That Portugee won't take his claws out of Ellen. He'll never let her go, till he's dead—and I'm going to attend to that. Get out of my way, Ed!" He rushed at Ed Race, thrusting at him with his shoulder.

Ed said regretfully, "I hate to do this, Tom, but it's the only way to save you from the chair!" With that, he brought up his knotted right fist in a short, well-timed uppercut that rocked Kirby on his heels, snapping his head back.

Tom Kirby's breath escaped with a long-drawn out *whoosh*, and his eyes became glazed. Ed had struck with the intention of knocking the acrobat out, and he had accomplished it. Kirby's knees buckled under him, and Ed caught him as he fell. Luckily, he had not pulled back the hammer of the revolver, and it didn't go off.

Ed lowered him gently to the floor, took the revolver out of his hand and put it back in the case. He locked the case. Then, with his eyes reflecting a bleak light, he stepped over Kirby and out into the corridor.

He saw Boiling, the assistant manager, and called to him, quickly explaining what had happened. Everybody in the theater knew about Ellen, and Boiling understood readily. "Take care of him," Ed told the assistant manager urgently. "And don't let him get away. Have a couple of the boys sit on him if necessary."

Boiling nodded. "Leave it to me, Ed. But what you going to do about it?"

"I'm going to talk to Esquibar!" Ed said grimly.

HE WENT outside and flagged a cab, drove up to Forty-eighth and Broadway. Gallipoli's Restaurant was just off Broadway, two doors down, on the opposite side of the street. Ed had his eye on the flashy plate-glass front of the eating-place as he paid off the taxi driver, and he didn't see Inspector MacSpain until the dour old inspector tapped him on the shoulder.

"What's the rush, Ed?" MacSpain demanded jocularly. "You got an appointment to kill a man?"

Ed turned and grinned at his friend. MacSpain was past fifty, but lithe and in excellent condition. His hair was all white, but the sparkle in his eyes indicated that his mind was as keen as a whip.

He looked shrewdly at Ed Race. "You generally eat at the Longmont Restaurant after the show, Ed. What brings you up this way tonight?"

Ed said hastily, "I've got to meet a man, Mac. Sorry, but I can't stay now. Drop in at the Longmont tomorrow, and I'll buy a drink—if you're off duty."

MacSpain grinned. "Okay, Ed. I'm browsing around the district tonight. May run into you later. There's a tip-off that a bundle of phony money is due to be put out pretty soon, and the Treasury people have asked us to spot any known passers. If you see any nineteen-thirty-six twenties with a Lincoln head, be careful. They were made from stolen plates, and are almost as good as the real stuff. The only flaw is a crack in the lower left-hand corner of the plate. It hardly shows up."

Ed nodded. "I'll be careful, Mac. See you tomorrow."

He left the inspector and hurried down Forty-eighth. He took a couple of steps, then stopped short. Carlos Esquibar was standing on his side of the street, with another man. They were both tensely watching someone or something inside of Gallipoli's Restaurant, directly opposite.

Ed faded into a doorway and kept his eyes on them. He remembered Carlos the Magician very well. The tall, sallow-faced Portuguese had not changed in the last few years. He was wearing a tan, belted topcoat, and a gray felt hat with a sloping brim. The other man was standing on the far side of Carlos, and Ed couldn't see him distinctly, but he could tell that the fellow was much shorter than Esquibar, and broad-shouldered.

It had been Ed Race's intention to find Esquibar and talk to him like a Dutch uncle. But now, seeing the tense, watchfulness of these two men, and noting that they both kept their hands in their coat pockets, Ed decided to wait a while.

He looked down the street past them, seeking the operative from the detective agency, who had 'phoned in to Tom Kirby. But he couldn't spot the man. He assumed that the operative would be well concealed.

Ed's forehead creased thoughtfully. Carlos and his stocky companion were up to something. They were interested in the restaurant across the street. Ed went back to the corner, crossed over, and strolled past the restaurant. It had begun to drizzle, and he pulled down his hat, turned up his coat collar. The chances were against Carlos recognizing him as he passed the lighted restaurant.

He slowed up as he passed the plate-glass window, peered in to see what was holding the interest of the Portuguese. Then his eyes suddenly narrowed. He recognized Ellen Kirby, sitting at a table near the window. She was alone, and apparently finishing a meal, for there was a cup of coffee and a small piece of pie before her.

Upon a sudden impulse, Ed turned in to Gallipoli's. He walked into the lighted restaurant and selected a table at the other end of the dining room from Ellen Kirby, but so placed that he had a view of the street.

HE ORDERED a cup of coffee, and studied Ellen Kirby. She would be twenty-one now. But she had lost none of her slim beauty, none of the lithe grace which had won the admiration of vaudeville audiences. Still, her face was a bit pinched, and Ed could see that there was tragedy in her eyes. She finished her coffee and pie and picked up the check. Her shoulders were sagging a bit as she put on her coat, and her step was listless as she made her way to the cashier's desk.

Ed Race threw a swift glance out the window. He saw Carlos Esquibar and his friend walking swiftly eastward, away from the restaurant.

He frowned thoughtfully, trying to figure the play. Ellen must still be living with Esquibar. Why, then, was Carlos following her? And if he *was* following her, why was he suddenly going away just as Ellen would be coming out?

Ed swung his eyes back to the cashier's desk and saw that Ellen was in some kind of trouble. The cashier, a fat man with a drooping mustache, was waving a bill at her, and talking fast, in a high-pitched, angry voice.

"Thisa money iss no good! She's a phony! You stay here. I call a cop!"

The cashier reached over and gripped Ellen's wrist, then

tapped a bell on the counter to summon Signor Gallipoli from the rear office.

Several of the patrons in the place turned to stare at the scene, and Ed Race got to his feet, went swiftly to the desk.

Ellen Kirby was standing there, with her wrist still in the grip of the cashier. Her face was frighteningly white, and she uttered a little gasp when she saw Ed Race. But she said nothing.

Ed said easily to the cashier, "What's that—a phony?"

The cashier glared at Ellen, waved the bill in the air. "She's a crook. She give me a phony twenty dollar!"

Ed said, "Huh. Let's see it."

He took the bill, looked closely at it. Sure enough, there was a minute crack running diagonally down the lower left-hand side of the bill. He raised the bill to the light, as if to look through it, and at the same time put his left hand casually in his trousers pocket. Ellen Kirby, still in the grip of the cashier, watched him with lackluster eyes.

Signor Gallipoli came puffing from the back of the store. He knew Ed Race, as did most of the businessmen along Broadway. Ed Race was the Masked Marksman, of vaudeville fame. He was billed from coast to coast on the far-flung Partages Circuit, as "The Man Who Can Make Guns Talk." His startling feats of well-nigh incredible marksmanship on the stage, with those six heavy .45 calibre hair-trigger revolvers, always left his audiences breathless with wonder.

But his restless nervous energy did not allow him to rest on the adulation of the crowd, or to be content with the enormous salary he drew down. The breath of excitement and danger was as necessary to him as were cigarettes to the average man. He had therefore, many years before, adopted a side-line—the profession of criminology. He held licenses to operate as a private detective in a dozen states; and he had as many friends in the police departments of scores of cities as he had enemies in the underworld. There was more than one occasion when he had befriended the businessmen of Broadway. Only a month ago they had tendered him a dinner and a gold watch. Gallipoli beamed at him, then scowled at Ellen Kirby, and turned inquiringly to the cashier, who explained volubly in Greek that she had offered him a counterfeit twenty-dollar bill—one which they had only today been warned against by the authorities.

Gallipoli said, "Hah! We catch the passer!" He glared at Ellen. "Wait till Inspector MacSpain get you in headquarters! You tell him who is your boss—no?"

Ellen looked helplessly at Ed, then said to Gallipoli, "But I didn't know—"

"Hah!" Gallipoli snorted. "Never does the passer know! Always is it a mistake! Call the police!"

"Wait a minute," Ed said mildly. "You don't want to go off half-cocked, Gallipoli. Better be sure this bill is a counterfeit before you have her arrested. She could sue you for damages, you know."

Gallipoli frowned and took the bill from Ed's hand. The cashier leaned forward eagerly, but not neglecting to keep his grip on Ellen's wrist. He began to spout Greek to his boss again, and pointed to the lower left-hand corner. Suddenly, he stammered, faltered, and grew red in the face. There was no crack in the lower left-hand corner!

Gallipoli studied the bill carefully, on both sides. His bushy eyebrows began to draw down ominously. He threw the bill on the counter and began to curse the cashier in fluent, stinging Greek. The cashier cringed under the verbal lashing. Ed Race stood by, without a trace of expression on his poker face. Ellen Kirby threw him a quick, grateful glance.

"That was fast work, Ed," she whispered.

Ed Race acknowledged her thanks with a short nod. He was busy with his left hand in his jacket pocket, stuffing the counterfeit twenty-dollar bill into the open package of cigarettes there.

Gallipoli was profusely apologizing, and thrusting the change of the twenty into Ellen's hands. The cashier was silent but still staring at the bill with a troubled expression, mingled with doubt. Whatever he thought, he kept quiet for fear of Gallipoli's anger.

ED PILOTED Ellen Kirby out of the dining room but put a hand on her arm while they were still in the vestibule.

"Tell me all about it now, Ellen," he said. "Carlos is out there with a friend."

She started, visibly. "Carlos! I—I thought he had gone! That man with him"—she shuddered—"is Franconi."

Ed raised his eyebrows. "Franconi? Who's he?"

She was trembling now, and there was the faintest trace of tears in her eyes. Ed put a heavy hand on her shoulder, steadied her. "Chin up, Ellen. You're in trouble, and I want to help you. Tell me about it. How come you're passing the queer?"

She looked up at him with wide, honest eyes. "I give you my word, Ed, I didn't know it was counterfeit. Carlos and I came into New York yesterday, from New Orleans. We—we took an apartment on Fifty-first Street. This man Franconi came and talked with Carlos almost all day, and Carlos made me stay in the bedroom while they talked. We—we hadn't eaten all day, because we had no money for food. Then Carlos came in, gave me the twenty-dollar bill, and told me to go to Gallipoli's and order a meal, and bring him back some sandwiches. He said he had to go somewhere with Franconi. He brought me here and left me, saying he'd meet me back at the apartment in a half-hour."

Ed saw that Ellen was on the verge of hysteria. He put an arm around her shoulders. "Why didn't you go to your father?" he asked her gently. "Tom would gladly help you, take you back. You don't have to stay with Carlos—"

Her chin came up.

"I made a mistake, Ed. I was a foolish kid, I suppose. But I'm not going to come crying on anybody's shoulder. I married Carlos, and I'm going to face it out. I—I couldn't go back to Dad, whipped—the way I am!"

A steely glint came into Ed Race's eyes. "All right, Ellen. You're a trouper, kid, and I'm not going to let you down.

Carlos must have this batch of counterfeit money. He gave you the twenty to try out, to see if it would go through. The rat—he didn't care if you were caught passing it!"

Ellen said, "I've taken about enough from him. I'm going

back and have it out. If he's handling this counterfeit money with Franconi, I'll—I'll turn him in!"

Ed thought swiftly. There were other ways to get at Carlos. He could tip off MacSpain, and the inspector could raid Carlos' apartment. But would he find the counterfeit money there? Perhaps Carlos didn't have it in the apartment. The raid would fall through, and Carlos would go free for lack of proof against him.

"Do you think you could locate the money?" he asked Ellen quickly.

"I'll try!" Her eyes were shining with sudden resolve now. "I've begged Carlos to let me have a divorce, but he only laughs at me. He says if I try to get one, he'll fight me through the courts—frame me, if he has to. He says he'll make my name a laughingstock all over the nation." She breathed deeply. "But if he's arrested and convicted for this, I could—could get a divorce."

Ed made up his mind. "All right, Ellen. It's the only way to do it. You go back. I'll follow you. Tell Carlos everything went off all right here. Tell him they took the bill without question. Show him the change to prove it. Then, if he goes out again, you search that apartment with a fine-tooth comb. See if you can find his hiding place. Locate that counterfeit money, and I'll get MacSpain to come in. That'll be better than his raiding cold, because it'll put you in the position of aiding the law. The other way, they'd look at you as an accessory!"

He gave her a few final instructions, and let her go out first. In a minute or two he followed her. He looked back to see the cashier watching him from inside. No doubt the man was wondering what they had been talking about, was becoming suspicious all over again. But Ed shrugged. He didn't care anymore what the cashier thought.

He had too many other things to figure. He hoped that Inspector MacSpain had not remained at the corner, for he didn't want any interference now. For Ellen's sake, he wanted to see this through without the intervention of the law, until he could get her clear of the whole thing.

And he hoped desperately that Boiling, the assistant manager of the Clyde Theater, had been able to keep Tom Kirby from going off on his lone manhunt. Ellen's father could ruin everything by butting in at the wrong moment.

ED GOT out into the street, and saw Ellen walking east, under a street lamp. His eyes quartered the block, and he caught sight of two shadowy figures in a doorway halfway up the block. That would be Carlos and his friend Franconi. Now Ed understood their action in walking away from Gallipoli's at the psychological moment. In the event that the counterfeit was discovered and Ellen caught, they didn't want to be too close to the restaurant when it happened. Their caution had worked out perfectly thus far, for they had been unable to see what transpired at the cashier's desk.

He fell in behind Ellen, keeping about two hundred feet behind her.

Ellen turned the corner at Sixth Avenue, and her two shadowers followed, crossing the street. Ed kept a good distance behind. She had given him the address of the apartment on Fifty-first Street, and he wasn't afraid of losing her. It was something else that worried him. Tom Kirby had told him that there was a detective agency operative shadowing Carlos, and Ed wanted to find that man.

It was not until they reached Fiftieth Street that Ed saw him. He was on the opposite side of Sixth Avenue, on the same side as Carlos and Franconi. Ed had seen him a block or so south, but hadn't been sure, because there were a number of other pedestrians out in the rain. Now Ed was sure, because the man had stuck all along.

Ed struck out diagonally across Sixth Avenue toward the operative, and the man saw him coming, elaborately turning to look into a pawnshop window.

Ed came up to him, and said, "Hello, Gerson!"

He knew the man. He worked for a shady outfit, known as the Red Star Agency, and Ed made a mental note to reprimand Tom Kirby for using such a disreputable firm. Gerson affected surprise. "Why, hello, Mr. Race! How's tricks?"

Ed could see that Gerson was throwing a nervous glance up the street at Carlos and Franconi, who were already turning into Fifty-first.

"It's all right, Gerson," Ed said. "I'm taking over. Kirby sent me instead of coming himself."

Gerson looked suspicious. "But Kirby said he'd be right over, when I 'phoned him—"

"I said I'm taking over," Ed told him coldly. "Do you want to argue?"

"No, no!" Gerson said hastily. He dropped his eyes. "It's okay with me, Mr. Race. I know you're a friend of Kirby's. That's his daughter, that just went around the corner—"

"Scram!" said Ed.

Gerson shrugged and slouched off.

Ed hurried around into Fifty-first Street. There was no sign of either Ellen Kirby, or of Carlos and Franconi. The address which Ellen had given him was a four-story brownstone about a third of the way up the block. Third floor front, she had said.

Ed walked past the house, looked up. There was no light in the third floor front, but he thought he saw a face at the window for a moment. The face disappeared at once, and the shade was pulled down. Then a light went on.

Ed was troubled. If Carlos had spotted him, there would be trouble. The Portuguese would be on guard, might even harm Ellen. Ed had told her that he would remain outside until he saw Carlos and the other come out, then he would follow them while she searched the apartment.

He waited ten minutes, and the longer he waited the surer he was that Carlos had spotted him. He began to have troubled thoughts of what the Portuguese and his friend might be doing to Ellen. Carlos the Magician had once worked the circus side-shows, but in the last few years no respectable midway would have him. He had opened booths in various cities, and had used his magic shows as a cover for numerous criminal enterprises. Carlos was a man without a conscience, and without compunction. If he suspected that Ellen Kirby was trying to get the goods on him, he would be equal to killing her.

His thoughts swept back over the years to the time when

Ellen, a little girl in pigtails, had first joined her father's acrobatic act. He remembered how she would swing from a low trapeze, close to the stage, hanging by her hands; how she would reach down with her bare feet, pick up a kewpie doll in those agile toes of hers, and then throw it with her feet to her father, who hung head down from the next trapeze. That number had been a knockout, and the Kirbys had toured America with it.

Now that demure little girl, who had won the love of every audience she appeared before, was upstairs with two criminals, one of whom was her husband!

Ed could wait no longer. He unbuttoned his topcoat, so as to have better access to his two shoulder holsters, and entered the dimly lit vestibule. There were only two or three names on the bells, and the name of Esquibar was not among them.

He started up the stairs, moving swiftly yet quietly. He reached the third-floor landing and paused a moment. There was no light at all on this floor, and he waited to accustom his eyes to the darkness. Four doors faced him, two at the rear, two at the front. From the position of the light he had seen in the window, he knew that the left-hand door at the front was the one he wanted. He began to move slowly toward it, and suddenly his blood was chilled by a pain-wracked moan that came from behind that door.

That was Ellen Kirby! He knew her voice, in spite of the agony that twisted her tones. He leaped for the door, his face tight and grim. He turned the knob, not expecting it to open. But it did. It gave under his pressure, and he pushed the door wide open.

At the same instant, something hard bored into his back. A voice behind him said, "Stand still, sucker!"

Ed Race, the blood running swift in his veins, stood rigid, with the gun at his back, and stared into the lighted apartment revealed by the open door.

IT WAS a combination dining-and-living room, with one of those old-fashioned round dining-room tables in the center. Upon this table stood an electric iron, plugged into the wall. The iron was glowing hot.

Beside the table, Ellen Kirby sat, strapped into a chair, arms twisted behind her. She had been secured with the straps from two valises which lay open and empty at the far side of the room. Ellen's shoes and stockings had been ripped off, and lay on the floor beside the chair. There were half a dozen large red blisters on her feet, where the hot iron had been applied. Her face was white, colorless, and her eyes stared at Ed with a deep, bottomless hopelessness.

Directly behind her, and sheltered by her body, stood Carlos the Magician, grinning at Ed Race. He had a gun in his hand, and was pointing it at Ed over Ellen's shoulder. "Come in, Señor Race," he said tauntingly.

Ed tensed, every fiber of his body ready to uncoil in sudden blinding action. Franconi, behind, nudged him with the gun. "Go ahead, sucker."

Ed Race went into the room, and Franconi kicked the door shut. Ed stood there and stared over Ellen's head at the sallow, smirking countenance of Carlos Esquibar. He said slowly, "I'm going to kill you for that, Carlos!" He jerked his head toward Ellen Kirby's blistered feet.

Esquibar showed perfect, white teeth in a grin. "Thees time, Señor Race, you weel not keel no one. Observe—I am behind Ellen. My friend is behind you. Do not try to draw those so-dangerous guns of yours, for I will surely shoot Ellen in the spine if you do. You do not weesh to see your best friend's daughter shot in the spine, no?"

Franconi laughed, behind Ed. "I guess you walked in, sucker. Carlos knew what he was talking about when he said you'd come up—alone!"

Ed said nothing. He measured his chances. He had often been in just as tight a spot. He knew that he could kick Franconi in the shin, and go into a back somersault as he did every night on the stage. He knew that, while his body was in whirling motion, these men would not be able to hit him, even in this small room. And finally, he knew that he could draw his two revolvers before he landed back on his feet, and shoot Franconi and Esquibar to death. He had done that trick every night on the stage for years, and was letter perfect in it—with the added difficulty of having to hit the flame of a candle at the other end of the stage, instead of the much easier target of a bulky man.

But he also realized that Esquibar fully intended to shoot Ellen the moment he started. Esquibar and Franconi would never have dared to buck him, even with naked guns, if they hadn't had Ellen there. Ellen's presence changed the picture.

Ed shrugged. "You win, Esquibar," he said flatly. "What do you want?"

Esquibar looked a little relieved. "We question my dear wife," he explained. "She have come in but two or three minutes before us, and she have somewhere hidden a so-valuable package of money. We cannot find it. We wish her to tell, but she is—what you call—stubborn!"

Ed said to her, "Tell them, Ellen."

She shook her head defiantly, even while she winced from the agony of her burned feet. "No! No!"

Esquibar shrugged. "Then we must proceed. You, Señor Race! You will take from your shoulder holsters your two guns, and put them on the floor. But remember—you will hold them with only two fingers while you put them down. Should you grab one in your whole hand, I will place a bullet in Ellen's spine!"

"Yeah," Franconi chimed in, nudging him with the gun. "And I'll blast *you!*"

Ed Race's eyes were suddenly narrowed and calculating. He opened his jacket, and very gingerly and carefully pulled out one of the guns, holding it between thumb and forefinger. Franconi moved over a little to one side, so he could see, and Carlos tensed, holding his gun muzzle between Ellen's shoulder blades.

Slowly, Ed put the gun down on the floor and shoved it over toward Carlos. Then he did the same with the second one. Both heavy revolvers came to rest near the chair in which Ellen sat. Carlos' eyes were glittering.

"So! The great and dangerous Ed Race is now disarmed. His teeth are drawn—he is no longer dangerous!"

Franconi stepped back a pace and kept Ed covered. "Get to work, Carlos," he muttered. "We want that dough."

Carlos said, "Ah, yes!" He stepped to the table and lifted the hot iron, tapped a thumb to it. "She will speak, I promise!"

Ellen's eyes were wide, fixed on that iron. She moaned, "Why did you give up your guns, Ed? They'll kill us both now. They'll never let us out of here alive once they get the money!"

Ed spoke to her in a flat, soft voice. "Do you remember that trapeze act you did when you were a kid—with your dad? That's why I gave up my guns."

CARLOS HAD holstered his own gun now, and he was coming around at the side of Ellen's chair, carrying the hot iron. He reached over and tore the dress from her breast, exposing the soft, white skin. "This time, Ellen dear," he snarled, "we try here. You can stand this maybe not so good as the feet—eh?"

Ellen Kirby didn't hear him. Her eyes were fixed, staring in sudden comprehension of what Ed Race had just said. His words had carried no significance for Carlos or Franconi. But to her they evoked memories—memories and a deep meaning.

Her eyes darted down to the two revolvers on the floor. Ed had given them up, in order to save her from being shot. But now, Carlos was not behind her with a gun. What Ed Race wanted was clear to her.

Carlos had one hand on her shoulder, and the other was bringing the sizzling iron toward the white skin of her breast. Ellen squirmed, as if trying to draw away from the searing heat. In reality she had slouched farther down in the chair. Her bare toes touched one of Ed's two guns. Neither Franconi nor Carlos noticed that, for Carlos' lustful eyes were on the iron, while Franconi kept his gaze glued to Ed.

With the same skill that she had used years before in picking up a kewpie doll while swinging from a trapeze, Ellen Kirby got her toes around Ed's gun, and lifted it. She made a convulsive motion with her body just as the hot iron touched her breast. She screamed, but she did not lose her presence of mind. She kicked the gun toward Ed Race.

Franconi had taken his eyes from Ed for the instant that Ellen screamed. The revolver went sailing through the air, but Ellen hadn't thrown it straight. It would pass four or five feet from where Ed stood. He bent his knees, leaped cleanly into the air after it.

Franconi cursed, and swung his gun around. But Ed Race already had his hand on the revolver. He let himself go through the air, throwing his body into a forward somersault.

Franconi shouted a mad curse and fired, but his slug gouged the wall at least two seconds after Ed had left that spot.

Ed's forward dive carried him into Carlos, whom he knocked backward. Carlos fell, tangled with the hot iron, and shrieked with pain and fear as the heated metal seared his flesh.

Ed was on the floor, his body twisting in a lightning motion.

Franconi fired again, but his shot was wild and frantic. It smashed the windowpane, sending a tinkling shower of glass down into the street. He didn't fire again. Ed Race shot once, from the crouch he had come into on the floor, and a huge black hole appeared on Franconi's forehead.

Ed didn't even wait to see where his slug had gone. He was too old a hand at this to worry whether or not he'd missed. He *knew* where he had hit Franconi.

He swiveled in time to see Carlos with his gun out, bringing it down into line with Ellen's bound figure. Ed's lips were a thin, tight, remorseless line as he touched the hair-trigger, sending a bullet straight into the white teeth of the Portuguese.

The heavy .45 calibre slug tore the top of Carlos' head off. The room resounded with the thunderous vibrations of the shooting.

Then Ed Race got to his feet, walked steadily over to Ellen's chair, began to unbuckle the straps. At the same time, the door from the corridor opened, and Inspector MacSpain barged in with his gun drawn.

MACSPAIN STOPPED short, gazing at the two bodies. "Holy mackerel, Ed," he exclaimed, "you worked fast! I followed you from the restaurant, and I gave you five minutes after you came up here. I guess it was four minutes too much!"

Ed grinned at him sourly. "Thanks for the escort, Mac. How come?"

MacSpain shrugged. "I passed Gallipoli's again, just as you came out. Gallipoli, himself, ran out and began to jabber about counterfeit money and such, and he pointed to you. I saw you were following a girl, and someone else was following her too, so I tagged along."

Ed Race nodded somberly. "Okay, Mac. You can tell your federal friends that they needn't worry about the counterfeit money anymore. I think we've cleaned that up." He glanced at Ellen.

She had shut her eyes to keep out the sight of the two dead men. A .45 calibre revolver will make a man very messy at close range. She touched the blister on her breast and winced. "The—

the money is all here, and the plates, too. They were in those bags."

MacSpain asked her eagerly, "But where are they now?"

She looked at Ed. "I hid the money and the plates—in the only place I could think of. I put them on top of the dumbwaiter and sent it to the roof!"

Ed grinned at her. "Good girl!" He went into the bathroom, and found a tube of salve. He came back and put some of it on her burns, while MacSpain pulled up the dumbwaiter and found the stacks of counterfeit money, as well as the plates.

"There's a reward for this," he said dubiously.

Ed smiled. "Half and half, Mac. Half to you, half to Miss Kirby."

"And you, Ellen," he said sternly, "go back to your dad. There's a spot waiting for you in that vaudeville act of his. From the way you slung me that revolver, you ought to be back in electric lights in no time."

She looked at him for a long minute, then suddenly covered her face with her hands, and great sobs wracked her body. Ed put an arm around her.

MacSpain winked at him over her shoulder. Then he looked around the room at Carlos and Franconi. "Why did you have to kill them so dead?" he asked.

Ed winked back solemnly. "I had to be sure Ellen would be a widow," he said.

TOP BILLING FOR MURDER

ED RACE thought nothing of it when young Jerry Talmadge asked him for a ten-dollar check in exchange for ten dollars cash. "I want to send it back home to mother," Jerry explained, "and I haven't got a checking account of my own."

"Okay, kid," Ed told him, smiling. "I'm glad to see you're settling down and thinking of your mother for a change. She's a grand old lady. If you quit trying to buck Lucky Linsey's roulette wheel, you'll have a lot more to send her."

Talmadge grumbled like a spoiled child. "Look, Ed, do I have to listen to a lecture in return for a favor? I'm old enough to know what I'm doing."

Ed shrugged. "All right. Only I thought I'd mention it. I hear you've been going over the hurdles at Linsey's place recently." He sat down and wrote the check, and Talmadge gave him the ten dollars.

That was Monday. On Thursday, Ed got the 'phone call from Mary Talmadge, Jerry's pretty little sister—the other half of the exhibition dance team of Talmadge and Talmadge. The call came in at the Clyde Theater, where Ed Race was rehearsing a new routine for his Masked Marksman act.

Mary sounded worried and frightened. "Ed, I've got to see you. It's about Jerry. He—he didn't show up last night, and I had to work at the Fountain Club with a substitute partner. I'm afraid he's in trouble."

Ed Race's hand tightened on the 'phone. His thoughts flew back to the ugly rumors he had heard in the last few days, about Jerry Talmadge's terrific losses to "Lucky" Linsey. "What kind of trouble, Mary?" he asked tightly.

"I—I don't know. I've called every place in town where he might be, but no one's seen him."

"Have you called the Club Linsey?"

"Yes. But the place hasn't opened yet. There wasn't anyone there but the cleaning people."

Ed glanced at his watch. "I'll be through with rehearsal in ten minutes. Where are you now?"

"I'm phoning from Miller's Theatrical Agency—on Forty-ninth, you know."

"Okay. Meet me at my bank in fifteen minutes. I have to get some cash. Then I'll buy you a drink, and we can talk about Jerry."

ED FINISHED the rehearsal in a preoccupied manner. He was worrying about Jerry Talmadge. Both Jerry and his sister were only a couple of kids who had been precipitated into the big Broadway money through the fortunate chance of winning a dancing contest back in their home state. Ed knew their mother, Lisette Talmadge, who had played the vaudeville circuits ten years ago, when Ed himself was just starting on his vaudeville headline career as the Masked Marksman—"The Man Who Can Make Guns Talk." That was the way he was billed on the Partages Circuits, from coast to coast, and it was no exaggeration. His marvelous feats of marksmanship with the six heavy

Ed Race fired, instantly!

.45 caliber revolvers, which were the props of his number, always left the audience literally breathless with amazement.

The most sensational routine of the act was the spot where he juggled all six of the guns, keeping them in the air, catching them one by one as they came down—firing each, when it came into his hand, at a row of candles thirty feet across the stage. People had been known to come night after night to his performance, in the hope of seeing him miss once. They were always disappointed.

As the highest paid one-man vaudeville act in the country, Ed Race had accumulated plenty of money, which he treated as carelessly as possible. He refused to be bothered with investments, and generally kept ten or fifteen thousand dollars on deposit. Anyone in the show business who was up against it financially could always count on Ed Race to have ready cash.

But Ed Race needed more than this measure of success to make life interesting. In order to provide an outlet for his surplus of nervous energy, he had found himself an avocation—criminology. He held licenses to operate as a private detective in a dozen states, and his uncanny ability with guns had often been at the service of friends in trouble—but without charge. Ed Race was as much feared and hated in the underworld as the Masked Marksman was admired by theater audiences.

He had promised Lisette Talmadge that he would look after her two kids till they got dry behind the ears in the Big Town, and now he was afraid that he had fallen down on that promise.

He rushed through the rehearsal, got into his street clothes, and slipped into his twin shoulder holsters two of the .45's without which he never went out.

IT WAS just inside the stage entrance that he saw Baldy Donovan. Baldy was peering furtively back toward the door, which was open, affording a view of Forty-sixth Street, and of the corner a few feet east. When he saw Ed Race, Baldy Donovan came hurrying over to him, motioning him away from the door.

"Gawd, Ed," he breathed, "I took an awful chance coming here!"

Ed raised his eyebrows. "You in a jam again, Baldy?" Two months ago he had helped Donovan to clear himself of a burglary charge. Baldy was a two-time loser already, and if he had been convicted he would have been put away for life.

Baldy kept looking out the door, and talking so fast that he slurred his words. "My Gawd, no, Eddie, I ain't in no jam. It's you that's in a jam!"

"Me? What did I do now—"

Donovan motioned impatiently with his hand. "Don't kid around about this, Eddie. I only picked up the dope this morning. The finger is on you, Eddie!"

Ed Race knew that the reformed safe-man didn't scare easily. If he was scared now, there must be something to it.

Baldy hurried on. "Somebody has hired Sammy Heller to knock you off. They're paying him five C's for the job, which is a damn good price. That cokey has been known to pop a guy for fifty bucks."

Ed's eyes narrowed. "Sammy Heller, eh? Who hired him?"

Baldy Donovan spread his hands in a futile gesture. "I couldn't get that, Eddie. All I know is, that Sammy Heller has been around in a couple of bars, asking about your habits, and when you rehearse, and where you eat. And he told Smitty, the barman at Groton's place that he was in the money because he was getting five hundred for a job today."

Ed put an affectionate hand on Donovan's shoulder. "You're

a good egg, Baldy. You're taking your life in your hands to tip me off."

The ex-yegg shuffled his feet embarrassedly. "Hell! Didn't you go to bat for me? I'd be some heel if I let you walk out in the street without warning that Sammy Heller was on the prowl for you!"

"Thanks, Baldy," Ed said sincerely. "I'll be careful."

Baldy hung back as Ed started for the door. "I better not be seen coming out with you. Now for God's sake, keep your eyes peeled. Heller knows you're poison with a gun yourself. He'll try to get you in the back."

Ed nodded, and started out. He hunched his shoulders slightly forward, to bring the butts of the two .45's into easier gripping position. He was wondering who had put the finger on him. True, he had made plenty of enemies in the past. But he couldn't think of anyone at this time to whom his life could be worth five hundred dollars. Ed might have notified the police to pick up Sammy Heller. But there were two things against that. First, he couldn't violate a confidence of Baldy Donovan. Baldy would forever be marked in the underworld as a stoolie. Secondly, even if he had Heller picked up, there was nothing to prove that he *intended* to commit murder.

Ed stepped out into the street, threw a quick glance in both directions, and started for Broadway. Forty-sixth was an east-bound express street, in which parking was prohibited; so he didn't have to worry about a slug in the back from a parked car. But traffic was moving east with him, and there was always the danger of Heller's driving up alongside him and letting go. Ed felt prickles in his spine until he turned into Broadway. Here the crowd was thicker, and even Heller would hesitate to blaze away.

It was only two blocks to the Citizen's Deposit National Bank. Mary Talmadge was already there, waiting for him, her face clouded with worry. When he saw her, Ed forgot about Sammy Heller and Baldy's warning. She was a slim, lithe young thing, with clear-blue innocent eyes that had not yet been clouded by the worldly sophistication of Broadway.

"Ed, if anything has happened to Jerry, I'll never be able to face mother," she said. "Jerry's been—well, a little wild lately. He—oh, Ed, he may even be dead!"

Ed Race put an arm around her, and patted her shoulder. "Chin up, kid. Jerry's old enough to take care of himself. Just because he didn't come home last night doesn't mean anything. A chap has a right to stay out once in a while." He said it, but didn't really mean it. He was terribly afraid that Mary was right.

With trembling hands she took an envelope out of her purse. "Here's a letter I found in Jerry's room. It was all stamped, and ready to mail to mother. It shows that Jerry intended to come back."

Ed glanced through it quickly. It was a short note. Jerry sent his love, said everything was okay, and then finished, "Next week is Aunt Nora's birthday, so I am sending you a check for ten dollars. Buy something she needs, and give it to her with my love. The last cash I sent you was lost in the mail, so I'm going to ask Ed Race for a check, and that should be safer...."

"You see," Mary Talmadge said, "Jerry just wrote the letter and then left it unsealed until he could get the check. He intended to come back—"

Ed said grimly, "He got the check. I gave it to him. But that was on Monday. You say he was back Tuesday night. Why didn't he mail it?"

Mary looked up at him miserably. "What'll we do, Ed? Shall I notify the Missing Persons Bu—*Look out!*"

Her warning came too late. Ed abruptly sensed someone standing close behind him. He started to turn, and felt something hard jammed against his right side.

A voice said, "Hello, Race. I hate to do this. But business is business. Get in that car at the curb—you *and* the dame."

ED GLANCED sideways, and saw the pinched features and pinpoint eyes of Sammy Heller. The man was a cocaine addict. He could act and look utterly normal, but no one could guess what fires of hell were raging inside that doped-up brain. Heller was grinning in most friendly fashion, and no one in the passing crowds suspected that he was holding a gun in Ed's back.

Mary Talmadge knew what was happening. She could see the mad readiness to murder in Heller's face, and she dared not utter a sound for fear that he would shoot at once.

Heller said pleasantly, "Don't start nothing, Race. I'd give it to the dame, just as easy." He jerked his head toward a sedan which had pulled in at the curb, driven by a sallow-faced Spick. "Get going."

Ed Race was taut, his muscles bunched and ready for action. He had been in tighter places in his life, and had fought his way out of them. Heller knew that. Heller had seen him perform on the stage, no doubt, observing how the Masked Marksman could go into a blindingly swift back somersault, and come out of it, shooting, with both .45's from his shoulder holsters. That was a feature number of Ed's act. And Heller, with the devilish ingenuity of his drug-stimulated brain, had chosen this moment, when he was with Mary Talmadge, to make his play. Ed would have taken a chance on smashing back with his elbow at Heller's gun, and then drawing his own gun while he flipped back in a somersault. But that man in the car might open fire, and Mary would surely get the slug.

His mouth became a thin, hard line. "All right, Mary," he said. "Let's do what Sammy says."

Moving very carefully, he took her arm and led her to the car. Heller came close behind him, following them into the rear seat. At Heller's direction, Ed sat at the far end, Mary in the middle, and Sammy on her right. No sooner were they in, then the car leaped forward.

Heller brought the gun out of his pocket, held it pointing at Mary. He grinned. "No hard feelings, Race. But the dame gets it the first minute you start to go for your guns."

Ed asked him mildly, "Don't you want me to give you my guns?"

Heller snickered. "Not a chance, Race. You keep your mitts on your lap where I can see them. I take no chances on you getting your paws near them cannons!"

The driver apparently knew exactly where to go. He wound expertly out of the Broadway traffic, and in ten minutes they were on the Henry Hudson Parkway, which runs north along the Hudson River edge, toward Van Cortlandt Park and the wide reaches of Westchester County.

Ed said, "If this is a bump-off, Sammy, why drag the girl into it? Let her out."

Sammy Heller looked really pained. "Geez, Race, I wish I could accommodate you. But you know how a twist will talk." He sighed regretfully. "I hate to do two jobs for the price of one. But in this business, we got to protect ourself."

Mary Talmadge was sitting between them, staring straight ahead, hands tightly clenched in her lap. Ed could see that she was thinking not so much of the quick death that was rolling toward her with each revolution of the wheels of the car—but of her mother at home, and how Lisette would take the news.

Ed himself was thinking hard. They were whizzing past Van Cortlandt Park, and out into the Saw Mill Road. There would be plenty of lonely spots around here where murder could be committed. Ed said to Heller, "Five hundred dollars is very little money for a job like this, Sammy. You can't be making much profit."

Sammy Heller shrugged. He kept the gun trained on Mary. "What the hell, Race, I've done jobs for a hell of a lot less. I made them ante up heavy for you, because there ain't many torpedoes in New York would tackle a guy with your rep."

"Who's paying you, Sammy?"

Heller only grinned. "Look, Race, how could I build up a good business if I blabbed about things like that? Them things is confidential between my clients and me. But I'm makin' a good profit on the job. The car is hot, so it don't cost nothin'. An my client is payin' Manuel there to drive it, so that don't come outa my end."

Manuel turned his head and looked back at them over his shoulder, smiling to show two rows of perfectly white teeth. "I t'ink you spikking to moch anyhow, Sammy. Thees, she's no tea-party."

Sammy Heller scowled. "Pipe down, Spick!" he growled. "You pay attention to your driving. That's where we turn—right up the road!"

Manuel lapsed into silence. A hundred feet farther, he swung off sharply to the right, into a dirt road that led up a hill toward an old, abandoned farmhouse.

Sammy Heller chuckled. "I got a regular system, Race. I own a acre of land up here. I bring all my jobs here, and bury 'em right on the spot. Saves the cops the trouble of finding the bodies."

Ed said, "You're quite a businessman, Sammy. Could I offer you a grand to cross your client?"

Sammy shook his head. "If you ain't got the dough on you, I could never trust you to pay off. And if you *have* got it on you, I'll get it off you anyway."

Ed glanced down slantwise at Mary Talmadge. He saw that she was holding herself together with a tremendous effort. He could understand how she felt, being inexorably faced with death within a matter of minutes.

MANUEL HAD stopped the car a hundred feet from the abandoned farmhouse. He got out and walked across to a patch of ground that was set off by a low chicken fence. In a cold, matter-of-fact manner he picked up a spade and began to turn up a small square of earth.

Sammy Heller suddenly lost all his geniality. He snarled, "All right, Race. Out!" He got up and turned so that he was facing both Ed and Mary. He kept his gun on them, while out of his left hand coat pocket he brought out a pistol with a silencer screwed to the barrel. It was with this latter weapon that he was going to do the killing.

Ed's eyes burned into Heller's. He dared not try anything now, for Heller would surely send a bullet into Mary's body in these close quarters. Ed leaned over and pulled back the handle of the door, so that it swung open. Then he bent and got out, backward, at Heller's direction.

"So I can see your hands!" Heller told him.

Ed stood just outside the car, in a half-crouch, while Mary climbed out. As soon as Mary was on the ground, he knew Heller would shoot. He saw the gunman inside the car tense, and his knuckles whiten on the silenced gun.

Ed didn't wait for Mary to get both feet on the ground. He lurched to one side, and gave her a hard shove that sent her sprawling to the right. At the same time, he dived to the left in a head-on somersault. They were both going in opposite directions now, and he counted on a split-instant of delay while Heller's brain settled on which one to shoot at first. Or, would the gunman fire both guns at the same time?

Ed didn't know how good Heller was. He, himself, could hit two targets at the same time, firing with both guns simultaneously. But there were few men alive besides himself who could do that. He gambled on Heller's not being one of them.

Ed's steel-springed body coiled into a ball, and he bent his head forward, landing smoothly on the back of his neck, rolling forward to come to his feet in as graceful and perfectly timed a somersault as anyone had ever seen on the stage. He heard two loud reports from Heller's guns, and felt the dirt kick up alongside him as he rolled.

He felt a surge of joy. Heller was firing both guns at him, ignoring Mary Talmadge for the moment. But Ed's body was a confusing, moving target, and Heller was shooting too fast. Those two shots were the only ones he got in, because, when Ed came to his feet facing the car, he had both big hair-trigger .45's miraculously in his hands—and both were roaring out their deep-toned messages of death.

The two, thundering slugs smashed the lead into Heller's body, one in the right shoulder, the other above the left elbow. Heller gurgled a half-screech, and dropped both guns as his body was literally flattened against the upholstery of the car by the savage force of the heavy-caliber bullets. It happened that quickly.

Ed swung easily toward where Manuel had dropped his spade in favor of a short-muzzled gun. But when Manuel saw Ed's still smoking revolvers turn their snouts toward him, he didn't want to fight it out. He bent low, and ran as fast as he could.

Ed shouted after him, "Stop! I'll shoot—"

Manuel yelled with terror, and kept running. Ed's lips tightened grimly, and he raised his right hand revolver for a snap-shot at Manuel's legs. But at that instant Talmadge picked herself up from the ground where Ed had flung her, and got directly in the line of fire.

With a low curse Ed held his finger away from the hair-trigger. Mary never knew how near she had come to death in that moment. Ed shouted to her, "Out of the way, Mary!"

She was dazed, but understood, and dropped to the ground. It was too late. Manuel had disappeared over a rise.

Ed Race shrugged, and holstered his revolvers. "Plenty of time to get that rat," he said. He went over and helped Mary Talmadge to her feet. "Take it easy, kid. Don't let the reaction get you."

She looked up at him with a forced smile. "D-don't worry about me, Ed."

"Good girl!" Ed gave her a squeeze, and led her back to the car. Sammy Heller was unconscious, bleeding like a pig. Ed tore off the gunman's coat and shirt, and made a crude bandage for his shoulder and arm.

"What are you going to do with him?" Mary asked.

"We'll take him along," Ed told her grimly. "When he comes to, he'll talk—or he doesn't get medical treatment!"

Mary's eyes opened wide. "You—you mean—you're not taking him to a hospital?"

"No!" Ed picked up Heller's two guns, wrapped them carefully in a handkerchief, and stowed them in a pocket of the car. "That'll be evidence, all right. I bet he's done all his killings with these two toys. Don't worry about him, Mary. Rats like this one seem to survive anything—but the electric chair. And he has to be made to talk. I want to know who paid him to gun me; and where Jerry is!"

"You think he knows that, too?"

"I'm sure of it. I'm convinced that this little stunt is connected somehow with Jerry's disappearance."

They both got in the front seat, and Ed turned the car around, drove it down the hill and on to the parkway, heading south toward the city.

TWENTY MINUTES' fast driving brought them back to Broadway and Forty-eighth, in front of the Citizens' Deposit National Bank. Ed took out one of his revolvers and gave it to Mary. "Put that in your purse, if it'll fit. Watch Heller. If he comes to, and starts yelling, don't be afraid to sock him. I don't want the police to get him till I've talked to him. I'm going in the bank. Remember."

He left her with the revolver, and strode in to the Citizens' Deposit. Lavery, one of the vice-presidents, saw the urgency in his face when he demanded to see his canceled checks at once. In two minutes he had the batch of them, and was thumbing through, with Lavery watching curiously.

Ed uttered a quick exclamation, and flipped one of the checks out of the bundle. He held it before Lavery's eyes. It was made out to Jerry Talmadge, and dated last Monday. But it was for ten *thousand* dollars!

"You see anything wrong with that check, Lavery?" he asked.

The vice-president took it, examined it closely. Suddenly his face became white.

"Good Lord, Mr. Race! It—it's been raised! I can see it now.

155

It's a beautiful piece of work. No wonder the teller passed it."
He turned the check over. "And besides, it came through the
Federal Reserve—deposited in the Fourth National, in the regular way. Our man wouldn't suspect anything—wouldn't think of
examining it closely."

"Even when it's for ten thousand dollars?"

Lavery raised his shoulders deprecatingly. "This is New York,
Race—and it's Broadway. We clear checks every day for ten
times this amount. Ten thousand isn't such a large sum—in a
bank."

Ed took the check from him, examined the endorsement. It
was duly endorsed by Jerry Talmadge, and underneath Jerry's
name was plainly written, *"For deposit only, to account of Mutual
Enterprises, Inc."*

Lavery was already on the 'phone, talking to the cashier of
the Fourth National, and making notes on a pad. Finally, he
said into the instrument, "Thanks. I guess you're stuck. If we get
a lead, I'll let you know. Better notify the Bankers' Protective."

He hung up and turned to Ed. "The cashier over at the Fourth
National says that this Mutual Enterprises was a dormant
account, opened about a year ago by a man named Bart Kelver.
It carried a small balance, but was never used until day before
yesterday, when this ten-thousand-dollar check was deposited.
The check cleared this morning, and at ten o'clock Bart Kelver
came in and closed out the entire account, drawing the ten
thousand in cash."

Ed said tightly, "Do they know who this Bart Kelver is?"

Lavery shook his head. "The account was opened in the ordinary way, and they required references. Kelver gave them the name of Manny Morgan, whose letter is on file recommending Kelver. Morgan is one of their depositors, who is in the loan business—"

Ed laughed harshly. "That's what the bank thinks. I know Manny Morgan. He's a bookie. And I know where to find him!"

Ed arose. "Thanks, Lavery. I'll see what I can dig up on this."

The vice-president looked up at him worriedly. "This isn't your headache, of course. The Fourth National is the one that's stuck, because they guaranteed the prior signatures automatically when they forwarded the check through the Federal Reserve. But we're also liable, because of our negligence in passing the raised check. But if you can lay your hands on this Kelver party—or whoever is behind him—and get back the ten thousand, I'm sure the Bankers' Protective would consider itself deeply in your debt."

"Maybe I can," Ed told him. "I've got another interest in this. Yesterday, a very nice kid—the one who endorsed that check—disappeared. This morning, I came within two seconds of being murdered."

Lavery's eyes opened wide. "Murdered!"

Ed nodded. "Don't you see? If I were dead, there would never be anybody to question that raised check. They'd have gotten away with ten grand—and without any fuss!"

He left Lavery staring after him, and strode out to the car. Mary Talmadge was waiting for him impatiently, in the back seat, keeping watch over the still unconscious Heller. Ed glanced down at the gunman's body, and frowned. "Wait here, Mary. I'll be back in two minutes."

HE LEFT her, walked down Broadway to Forty-seventh, and went into a cigar store. A short, stocky man was in the 'phone booth, writing something on a sheet of paper. Ed pushed the door of the booth open, and heard the stocky man say, "That's Sister Susie in the second at Jamaica, ten to win and ten to show. Right, Mr. Marklewiczh. Thanks for the business. I'll take care of it for you."

The man hung up and said, "Hello, Ed. Ain't seen you for weeks. Want to give me a bet?"

Ed took him and led him into the rear of the store. "Look, Manny, I want some information. I want it quick, and I want it straight."

Manny Morgan took one look at his tense face, and said, "Sure, Ed. Anything you want to know—for you."

"This is something the cops will be asking you about in a little while, too."

Manny Morgan's eyes narrowed. "The cops couldn't get a thing from me, Ed. I'd never talk to them in a million years. You know what my life would be worth here on Broadway if I stooled. If you want to know anything, you got to gimme' your word that you don't pass it on to the cops. Otherwise—no soap."

Ed said impatiently, "All right, Manny, I give you my word. Now this is what I want to know. About a year ago you gave a reference to a man named Bart Kelver, who wanted to open an account in your bank."

Manny Morgan's forehead creased in thought. "Bart Kelver?

I don't remember...." Suddenly, he snapped his fingers. "Sure! That was...." He broke off abruptly, gave Ed Race a queer look. "Say, Ed, what's in back of it?"

"So far, Manny, it's only forgery and attempted murder. Maybe it'll be actual murder before it's over."

Morgan lowered his voice. "Look, Ed, I wouldn't mix in this if I was you. This is dynamite."

"I'll say it is!" Ed told him. "I was almost taken for a ride this morning."

Morgan whistled. "Holy mackerel! You! What's Linsey got against you?"

Ed Race gripped the bookmaker's shoulder. "Did you say *Linsey?*"

Manny Morgan nodded. "Believe me, Ed, I wouldn't open up to anyone but you. That Bart Kelver—it's just a stooge name for one of Linsey's accounts. He's got a couple dozen accounts like that, all over town. He gets friends to recommend them, so he wouldn't be tied up with them. He always keeps a couple of these accounts in reserve, in case he gets a strange sucker at his wheels, who drops a lot of dough. Then if the sucker squawks later, it can't be tied to Linsey."

Ed said slowly, "Then there isn't any Bart Kelver?"

"Sure. Kelver's probably one of Linsey's gorillas. He's got accounts and safety boxes in all their names."

"Thanks, Manny," Ed said. "You don't need to worry. I won't talk to the police about this. If I get Linsey, it won't be by using your information."

"That's why I opened up to you, Ed. I know you're a right guy. And Linsey hasn't got any business tangling with a guy like you."

Ed left Morgan and strode out of the cigar store. He hurried back to the car, and Mary Talmadge's eyes sought his eagerly. "Any news of Jerry, Ed?"

Ed glanced down at Heller, saw that the gunman was still out. The bandages weren't bleeding. If gangrene didn't set in, he'd be all right.

"I think I know where Jerry is," Ed told her. "I want you to stay right here and watch Heller. I don't know how long I'll be gone. If I don't come down in twenty minutes, I want you to call the traffic cop from the corner and turn Heller over. Also, tell the cop that I've gone over to the Club Linsey, and that there may be trouble there. Tell him to notify Inspector MacSpain."

Mary Talmadge clutched at his sleeve. "Ed! You're going into some terrible danger, and all because of Jerry—"

"I'll be all right!" he told her grimly.

HE LEFT her, went to the corner and crossed Broadway toward a low three-story building on the other side of the street. There was an electric sign across the face of the building. It wasn't working now, wouldn't be turned on until the evening. But the lettering could be easily read, nevertheless—*Club Linsey*.

The ground floor was an elaborate restaurant with a four-dollar floor show. Upstairs were the private gaming-rooms run by Lucky Linsey, as well as his office. Ed looked up, caught the quick shifting of a face in one of the windows of the second floor. He had to look down again in order to dodge traffic across Broadway, and when he raised his eyes again, the face was gone.

Ed's mouth tightened. He had been under observation all the time that the car had been parked there in front of the bank.

He plowed through the crowds in the street, entered the wide lobby of the restaurant, and turned left to a private elevator which gave access to the upper floors. A heavy-set, thick-jowled man ran the elevator. He was standing in the open doorway of the cage, watching Ed with a blank expression on his unemotional face. His features did not move, except for his thick lips, which were sliding a toothpick from right to left, then back again from left to right.

Ed said to him tightly, "I'm going up to see Linsey, Butch. Do you want to take me up, or do I have to take you?"

Butch took the toothpick out of his mouth. "Hell, there won't be no trouble goin' up, Race. Mr. Linsey's expectin' you!"

Ed's eyes narrowed. But he asked no questions. He let Butch step into the cage, then followed him. Butch sent the elevator up to the next floor, brought it to a stop at the landing. Before he could slide the door open, Ed said sharply, "Butch!"

The big man turned around. "Yeah?"

Ed said, "Sorry. I got to have my back-trail clear," and he hit Butch on the point of the jaw with all he had.

The man's eyes popped. He let a feeble grunt escape from his sagging mouth, and slid gently down along the wall to rest on the floor. Ed bent down and took a gun out of the man's shoulder holster, put it in his own empty left-hand one, to replace the gun he had given Mary Talmadge. Then he opened the cage door and stepped out onto the second floor.

There was nobody in the corridor. Lucky Linsey's private

office was directly opposite the elevator. Farther down the hall were the gambling-rooms, but these were deserted at this early hour of the day. Later, when the night life of the city woke up, those rooms and this corridor would be full of men and women, and hurrying waiters. The drone of the croupiers' voices would be clearly audible out here. Now, however, all was quiet.

Ed crossed the hall, and pushed open the door of Linsey's office with his left hand. His right was close to his shoulder holster.

He walked into the room. There had been voices a moment ago, but now there was sudden silence.

Lucky Linsey sat a broad streamlined modernistic desk facing the door. A thin little wisp of a man sat at his left. A tall, gaunt man with hunched shoulders was standing at Linsey's right. A door at the right was ajar, revealing another room, where someone was moving about.

ED RACE kicked the corridor door shut behind him. He knew the little man at Linsey's left. He kept his eyes locked with Linsey's, but he spoke to this one. "So Scribbler Harris is writing paper again! Scribbler, you scribbled yourself into a ten-year pen stretch when you raised that check of mine!"

Linsey didn't say a word. He was a well-set-up man of forty. Immaculately dressed in a pinstripe blue suit, with shirt, tie and handkerchief to match, he sat with his well-manicured hands on the desk, and his black eyes burned into Ed's. But the gaunt man with the hunched shoulders stirred, and his hand rose a little toward his armpit. It was only then that Linsey spoke, in a flat, unemotional, gambler's voice. "Take it easy, Kelver."

The man stopped the upward movement of his hand.

But Ed had heard that name. He tensed. This was the one who had deposited the raised check in the Fourth National.

Scribbler Harris whined, "I don't know what you're talking about, Race. I never raised no check of yours—"

Linsey said, "Shut up, Harris!"

The old forger lapsed into silence.

Ed kept his eyes on the gambler. "Linsey," he said softly, "I'll give you two minutes to produce Jerry Talmadge—alive."

Linsey kept his hands on the table. "You're a fool, Race. You'll gain nothing by using those guns of yours—except a murder rap. You broke in here. There are no weapons in sight."

Ed Race said, "Fifty seconds gone. Seventy seconds to go."

Linsey said, "We don't know a thing about it. The Talmadge kid lost ten grand here, and gave us your check for that amount—"

"That's a lie," Ed told him. "Jerry Talmadge may be wild, but he's not a crook. And he didn't have the skill to raise that check. He dropped the ten-dollar check at your tables, and you saw your chance to clean up. And you hired Sammy Heller to take me for a ride, so there'd be no one left to squawk." He looked up at the electric wall clock above Linsey's head. "Ten seconds to go."

Scribbler Harris was shivering. Kelver shifted surreptitiously, his hand traveling another inch toward his armpit. Five seconds ticked off in utter silence.

Then Linsey said, with no change of expression on his gambler's face, "You win, Race. I'll get you Talmadge." He raised his voice. "Mac! Bring the Talmadge kid in. *Understand?*"

A man in the next room answered, "I get you, boss!"

In a moment, the man appeared in the doorway connecting with the next room. He was holding Jerry Talmadge up in front of him. Jerry's mouth was taped, and his hands tied behind him. And the man who held him was shoving a gun out in front of Jerry's body, pointing at Ed Race.

Linsey said quickly, "Give it to him, Mac!"

Ed Race dropped to the floor. Mac's gun thundered, and a slug whined over Ed's head. Ed rolled over twice, and came to his knees with his .45 belching thunder. His first shot, fired while he was still practically in motion, shaved the tip of Jerry Talmadge's ear and smashed into Mac's face. Kelver's gun was out, but Ed threw himself forward and shot from his prone position. The slug took Kelver in the throat, and literally carried off the top of his head.

Scribbler Harris was under the desk yelling for mercy, and Lucky Linsey was standing up, with his hands raised in the air. He was saying something, but Ed couldn't hear him because the thunder of the gunfire was still reverberating in the room.

Ed kept him covered, and went over and pulled the tape off Jerry Talmadge's mouth. It came off with a ripping noise, and Jerry winced. He twisted his lips to get the circulation going, then said, "God, Ed, I was slated for the ash heap. Sammy Heller was scheduled to take me for a ride when he finished with you. This was the pay-off. Kelver brought up the ten thousand to split with Linsey and Harris. I think you'll find the money in his pocket."

Ed said, "You damn fool kid, will you quit gambling?"

"I will, Ed," Jerry said earnestly. "I'll never so much as put a nickel in a slot machine!"

Ed went to the window and looked out on Broadway. In front of the bank, Mary Talmadge was excitedly talking to a policeman, and pointing up to the window. He smiled. "Mary didn't wait twenty minutes. The Marines will be here soon." He looked at Scribbler Harris, who was crawling out from under the desk, then at Lucky Linsey. "I guess your luck has run out Linsey. If Heller doesn't talk, Harris here, certainly will. How's that?"

Linsey shrugged. "I should have known better than to pick you for a sucker, Race. The thing that hurts is that Sammy Heller took me to a shooting gallery and knocked off a whole row of candles with a gun, to prove to me he could take you!"

Ed grinned at him. "The trouble is," he told Linsey, "that the candles didn't do somersaults while he was popping at them!" He laughed now.

THE SPIDER

- ❏ #1: The Spider Strikes — $13.95
- ❏ #2: The Wheel of Death — $13.95
- ❏ #3: Wings of the Black Death — $13.95
- ❏ #4: City of Flaming Shadows — $13.95
- ❏ #5: Empire of Doom! — $13.95
- ❏ #6: Citadel of Hell — $13.95
- ❏ #7: The Serpent of Destruction — $13.95
- ❏ #8: The Mad Horde — $13.95
- ❏ #9: Satan's Death Blast — $13.95
- ❏ #10: The Corpse Cargo — $13.95
- ❏ #11: Prince of the Red Looters — $13.95
- ❏ #12: Reign of the Silver Terror — $13.95
- ❏ #13: Builders of the Dark Empire — $13.95
- ❏ #14: Death's Crimson Juggernaut — $13.95
- ❏ #15: The Red Death Rain — $13.95
- ❏ #16: The City Destroyer — $13.95
- ❏ #17: The Pain Emperor — $13.95
- ❏ #18: The Flame Master — $13.95
- ❏ #19: Slaves of the Crime Master — $13.95
- ❏ #20: Reign of the Death Fiddler — $13.95
- ❏ #21: Hordes of the Red Butcher — $13.95
- ❏ #22: Dragon Lord of the Underworld — $13.95
- ❏ #23: Master of the Death-Madness — $13.95
- ❏ #24: King of the Red Killers — $13.95
- ❏ #25: Overlord of the Damned — $13.95
- ❏ #26: Death Reign of the Vampire King — $13.95
- ❏ #27: Emperor of the Yellow Death — $13.95
- ❏ #28: The Mayor of Hell — $13.95
- ❏ #29: Slaves of the Murder Syndicate — $13.95
- ❏ #30: Green Globes of Death — $13.95
- ❏ #31: The Cholera King — $13.95
- ❏ #32: Slaves of the Dragon — $13.95
- ❏ #33: Legions of Madness — $12.95
- ❏ #34: Laboratory of the Damned — $12.95
- ❏ #35: Satan's Sightless Legion — $12.95
- ❏ #36: The Coming of the Terror — $12.95
- ❏ #37: The Devil's Death-Dwarfs — $12.95
- ❏ #38: City of Dreadful Night — $12.95
- ❏ #39: Reign of the Snake Men — $12.95
- ❏ #40: Dictator of the Damned — $12.95
- ❏ #41: The Mill-Town Massacres — $12.95
- ❏ #42: Satan's Workshop — $12.95
- ❏ #43: Scourge of the Yellow Fangs — $12.95
- ❏ #44: The Devil's Pawnbroker — $12.95
- ❏ #45: Voyage of the Coffin Ship — $12.95
- ❏ #46: The Man Who Ruled in Hell — $13.95
- ❏ #47: Slaves of the Black Monarch — $13.95
- ❏ #48: Machineguns Over the White House — $13.95
- ❏ #49: The City That Dared Not Eat — $13.95
- ❏ #50: Master of the Flaming Horde — $13.95
- ❏ #51: Satan's Switchboard — $13.95
- ❏ #52: Legions of the Accursed Light — $13.95
- ❏ #53: The City of Lost Men — $13.95
- ❏ #54: The Grey Horde Creeps — $13.95
- ❏ #55: City of Whispering Death — $13.95
- ❏ #56: When Thousands Slept in Hell — $13.95
- ❏ #57: Satan's Shakles — $14.95
- ❏ #58: The Emperor From Hell — $14.95
- ❏ #59: The Devil's Candlesticks — $14.95
- ❏ #60: The City That Paid to Die — $14.95
- ❏ #61: The Spider at Bay — $14.95
- ❏ #62: Scourge of the Black Legions — $14.95
- ❏ #63: The Withering Death — $14.95
- ❏ #64: Claws of the Golden Dragon — $14.95
- ❏ #65: The Song of Death — $14.95
- ❏ #66: The Silver Death Reign — $14.95
- ❏ #67: Blight of the Blazing Eye — $14.95
- ❏ #68: King of the Fleshless Legion — $14.95
- ❏ #69: Rule of the Monster Men — $16.95
- ❏ #70: The Spider and the Slaves of Hell — $16.95
- ❏ #71: The Spider and the Fire God — $16.95
- ❏ #72: The Corpse Broker — $16.95
- ❏ #73: The Spider and the Eyeless Legion — $16.95
- ❏ #74: The Spider and the Faceless One — $16.95
- ❏ #75: Satan's Murder Machines — $16.95
- ❏ #76: The Spider and the Pain Master — $16.95
- ❏ #77: Hell's Sales Manager — $16.95
- ❏ #78: Slaves of the Laughing Death — $16.95
- ❏ #79: The Man From Hell — $16.95
- ❏ **NEW:** #80: The Spider and the War Emperor — $16.95

THE WESTERN RAIDER

- ❏ #1: Guns of the Damned — $13.95
- ❏ #2: The Hawk Rides Back from Death — $13.95
- ❏ #3: Gun-Call for the Lost Legion — $13.95
- ❏ #4: The Law of Silver Trent — $13.95
- ❏ #5: The Gun-Prayer of Silver Trent — $13.95
- ❏ #6: Silver Trent Rides Alone — $13.95

CAPTAIN SATAN

- ❏ #1: The Mask of the Damned — $13.95
- ❏ #2: Parole for the Dead — $13.95
- ❏ #3: The Dead Man Express — $13.95
- ❏ #4: A Ghost Rides the Dawn — $13.95
- ❏ #5: The Ambassador From Hell — $13.95

DR. YEN SIN

- ❏ #1: Mystery of the Dragon's Shadow — $12.95
- ❏ #2: Mystery of the Golden Skull — $12.95
- ❏ #3: Mystery of the Singing Mummies — $12.95

THE MASKED MARKSMAN

- ❏ #1: Death Takes an Encore — $16.95
- ❏ #2: Death's Understudy — $16.95
- ❏ #3: Death Steals the Act — $16.95
- ❏ **NEW:** #4: Top Billing for Murder — $16.95